"Please leave my shop!" Gwynneth demanded of the arrogant Lord Langley.

Langley's handsome face flushed with anger. He grabbed her by the shoulders. "You want conduct, Miss Dunlevvy. If you were a man, I'd take a horsewhip to you. As it is . . ." He paused, and looked down at her. A change came over his features. "As it is, I shall have to think of a punishment more suitable for a woman."

His hands began moving up and down her arms, pressing her soft body between his hard, muscular one and the door to the shop. Gwynneth felt dizzy with the scent of him, a devastating mingling of spice, expensive cloth, leather, and healthy vigorous male . . . the feel of him . . . the superbly sensuous mouth descending toward her own.

She was filled with rage, too—not at this maddeningly masterful male—at her own weakness. She had to find a way to hide the sparks of anger that lit a far more fearful flame between them. . . .

The Baron and the Bookseller

by

June Calvin

A SIGNET BOOK

SIGNET
Published by the Penguin Group
Penguin Books USA Inc., 375 Hudson Street,
New York, New York 10014, U.S.A.
Penguin Books Ltd. 27 Wrights Lane,
London W8 5TZ, England
Penguin Books Australia Ltd. Ringwood,
Victoria, Australia
Penguin Books Canada Ltd, 10 Alcorn Avenue,
Toronto, Ontario, Canada M4V 3B2
Penguin Books (N.Z.) Ltd. 182–190 Wairau Road,
Auckland 10, New Zealand

Penguin Books Ltd, Registered Offices:
Harmondsworth, Middlesex, England

First published by Signet, an imprint of Dutton Signet,
a division of Penguin Books USA Inc.

First Printing, August, 1994
10 9 8 7 6 5 4 3 2 1

To my husband, Donald Wayne Calvin, who had such strong faith that I would one day be published, and who was willing to invest the time and money necessary to make that possible; and to Dorothy Compton, a fellow writer who got me started reading and writing romances, and who kept me going through her encouragement and example. Thanks, Mom!

Chapter One

The door to the bookshop opened with a bang that drowned out the tinkle of the bell. Startled, Gwynneth nearly lost her footing on the stepladder she was using to dust the top shelves. She turned as booted feet moved authoritatively across the shop. A tall, expensively dressed gentleman strode toward her.

"May I be of service, sir?" She hopped off the stepladder and found herself looking up, way up, into a frowning, intense countenance.

"I would speak to Mr. Dunlevvy."

She drew in a quick, composing breath. "Mr. Dunlevvy is deceased, sir, these six months."

The gentleman rocked back on his heels a bit, contemplating the ceiling. "Ah, the proprietor, then, whomever he may be."

"I am the proprietor, or proprietress, as you will, sir. How may I help you?"

He really looked at her for the first time. "Stap me! A chit of a girl is M. Dunlevvy, Bookseller?" His eyes held a derisive gleam. "Are you widow or daughter to the late Mr. Dunlevvy?"

He was surely a creditor. An unknown creditor come to shake the last of her tiny capital from her purse and seize her livelihood. But she answered him calmly, her small firm chin up. "Daughter, sir. If you would state your business?"

Curtly, the tall, dark-haired man responded, "I am Lord Langley. If you are indeed the proprietress of this establishment, you are aware that I send mail here, in care of M. Dunlevvy, for a certain Miss Allen. Do you receive this correspondence?"

Gwynneth's pale face went even whiter at learning the identity of her imposing visitor. But her voice was cool and composed as she responded, "Yes, Lord Langley, I receive and forward Miss Allen's mail."

"Forward?" His eyes narrowed. "I was under the impression she lives here in Guilford." An instant of consideration brought a sudden alteration in the tall man's manner. Suddenly he became friendly and confiding. "You look an understanding, kindhearted girl. I am most eager to meet Miss Allen in person, but she is very shy. You'll help me meet her, won't you? I'll be eternally grateful." He took her hands and drew her toward him, looking pleadingly, soulfully into her eyes. Gwynneth felt her heart accelerate, and her lips seemed somehow to tingle.

She looked quickly down and away, and pulled her hands from his to smooth her apron, willing her heart not to pound its way out of her chest. How much better it would be if Papa were alive to deal with this inevitable confrontation. He had warned her this dangerous day would come. And from the arrogant and rakish assurance of Lord Langley's manner, it was every bit as dangerous as he had warned her. In fact, even more so now that she was alone. When she had first begun the deception, her father had been alive to advise and protect her.

She stood mute. Finally Lord Langley's deep voice rumbled, "Come, sweet one, answer me and do a great service to Miss Allen and yourself."

"You know I cannot. I am not at liberty to discuss anything about Miss Allen." She raised her eyes, looking at him steadily.

"Including her real name, I assume?" His voice had

grown less friendly. The full, shapely mouth turned down with irritation.

Again she stood mute. "I will make it worth your while . . . " He reached inside his riding jacket and began to draw out a leather purse.

Gwynneth took a step backward, moving her hand in a negative gesture. "Do not, I beg you. I will not accept it."

Lord Langley turned abruptly and stalked toward the door. On the threshold he stopped, hesitated, and then turned back. "Would paper and ink be available in this benighted shop?" His voice was a snarl now. "And sealing wax."

Gwynneth quickly provided him with supplies, then continued her dusting while watching him surreptitiously as he sat at a table, writing rapidly.

She had heard that he was handsome. His reputation in this was true. His hair was longer than the fashion. The indifferently styled dark brown locks curled about his long, strongly chiseled face. He had heavy, high-arched eyebrows above eyes so dark brown they seemed almost black. The long, straight nose and generous, firmly cut mouth were set in a severe long face deeply cleft by vertical lines at the mouth. Laugh lines, perhaps? But surely shaped as well by the less pleasant passions such as irritation and anger. Whatever their origins, they made him look older than the thirty-two years she knew him to have in his dish.

His clothes were clearly of the finest material, but comfort had been taken into account to an unfashionable degree, for the jacket lay loosely across his broad shoulders, and his breeches above his riding boots admitted a few wrinkles rather than hugging his muscular thighs like a second skin. This was in accord with Lord Langley's published contempt for clothing that made the wearer uncomfortable.

The boots were masterpieces that the most aspiring dandy would have treasured, however, and gleamed even in the dim light of the shop. They encased long calves sprawled inelegantly under the table.

Gwynneth's heart still seemed an untamed creature as she absorbed the elemental attractiveness of this excitingly masculine man.

Papa's words suddenly rang in her ear. "I will permit this correspondence on the promise you will never reveal your name to him. He is handsome and has the reputation of being a rake. Certainly he has all the arrogance of the titled and wealthy. Add that to his intellect, and he would be what you, innocent and unsophisticated, might not be able to resist. And should he choose to act the rake, I would not be sure to be able to protect you from such a powerful man."

Now even such meager protection as her father could give her was gone. Gwynneth started as Langley rose abruptly from the chair and advanced on her with the sealed note in his hand. "See Miss Allen gets this as usual," he snapped brusquely, shoving it into her hand.

Lord Langley watched as she carried the letter solemnly behind the counter and deposited it in a small chest that she carefully locked. He felt no hesitation in taking the opportunity to study and assess her, as he would any nubile female.

He took in the well-shaped, proudly carried head and the tall, slender body, pausing in his survey to notice approvingly the deep, well-rounded bosom. She was somewhat above the average woman in height, but no Long Meg.

Hair pale and fine as corn silk had been scraped into a severe bun from which tiny straggling wisps escaped in a shining halo around her head. Her tiny cap was unattractive, an old maid's cap as dowdy as the shabby high-necked black bombazine dress she wore. Her face was oval, her fair complexion smooth but lightly dusted on the short, straight nose with barely visible freckles.

Ambiguously colored eyes were fringed generously with

light brown lashes. He had already taken note of those large, round eyes—hazel, he supposed they would be called, but in truth almost yellow in color.

Interesting. Taken separately, rather undistinguished features. Certainly not a diamond, yet attractive, with a most tempting body, he decided. And so prim and proper! Her sort of cool propriety was almost a challenge to a man to do his best—or was it worst?—to overset her.

The young woman's task complete, she turned to discover his assessing stare. "When do you think she will receive that?" He didn't trouble to hide his insolent interest.

"I couldn't say, my lord." Though Gwynneth flushed slightly under his improper scrutiny, she remained aloof.

"Couldn't, or won't?" He snorted at her stubbornness. "See she gets it as soon as possible. I am in some hurry for the response. I am staying for a few weeks with Mr. Nicholas Verleigh. Do you know him?"

Her cool nod set his back up. Acts as if she were the queen conducting a drawing room, he thought irritably. "Send word to me there when it arrives." He tossed a coin down on the table and turned to walk away.

Gwynneth looked at the gleaming golden round with startled eyes. A guinea. It was too much.

"There's no need . . . " This cavalier flaunting of his wealth rankled. She hurried rapidly toward him, the coin in her outstretched hand.

"Take it." His eyes ran dismissively over the shop, noting the lack of customers. "You obviously don't make much here. Selling books, at least. Perhaps in addition to forwarding clandestine correspondence, you have *other* sources of revenue." He arched an eyebrow insinuatingly. *That* ought to set the prim, cool young miss's back up.

Infuriated, Gwynneth grabbed his hand and forcefully shoved the coin into it. "I don't want it. And I don't want you with your arrogant insults in my shop again!" Her eyes darkened, flashing with fury. She bounded to the door and opened it, motioning him out.

Lord Langley's usually fashionably pale visage flushed red with anger. In a trice he slammed the door shut again and grabbed her by the shoulders, shaking her furiously. "You want conduct, Miss Dunlevvy. If you were a man, I'd take a horsewhip to you and teach you how to conduct yourself with your betters. As it is . . . "

He paused to study the badly shaken girl. The mobcap had flown off, and her hair had come tumbling in silken disarray around her face. Her full bosom pushed against the confinement of her dress as she gasped with fear and anger. The attraction he had felt to this girl from the moment he set eyes on her flared into irresistible life.

A change swept over his features. The gleam in his eyes was appreciative and diabolically suggestive. "As it is . . . I shall have to think of a punishment more suitable to a woman."

His hands gentled and began moving up and down her arms as he advanced on her, pressing her soft body between his hard, muscular one and the door to the shop. "Perhaps a kiss?" His voice coaxed, his eyes enticed. "One kiss, and all is forgiven."

"No! Leave me alone," Gwynneth sputtered, trying to push him away. As well push on a stone wall, for all the effect it had. The rush of awareness of him that assaulted her senses made her as dizzy as the shaking had: The scent of him, a devastating mingling of spice, expensive cloth, leather, and healthy vigorous male; the feel of him, his body so firm where it pressed against her softness; the sight of those drowning-pool brown eyes gleaming with desire; the husky, slightly gravelly sound of his voice coaxing her for a kiss; the devastatingly sensuous mouth descending toward her own.

"I said no!" She forced the words from lips grown strangely unwilling to utter them.

Langley caught her hands and lifted them over her head, pinioning them to the wood with his strong left hand. He lowered his head, chuckling, a deep masculine rumble that she could feel vibrating in his chest as it pressed against her. There was something in those dark-fringed brown velvet eyes that mesmerized her.

Gwynneth's impotent rage at being so completely trapped was accompanied by another, very contradictory, sensation. The hard masculine body pressed against her seemed somehow to cause her own to vibrate with excitement. She ceased her struggles. Time hung suspended as she watched the purposeful downward descent of his firm mouth.

"No!" At the last moment she managed to turn her head away. His lips made contact with her jawline, and he began to explore her skin, nibbling at her in a way that sent deep shivers through her. Ignoring her struggles, he persisted in his leisurely exploration of her face. At the same time, his free right hand moved between them to mold the curve of her bosom. Boldly he outlined her ear with his tongue.

A shudder ran through her, but it was not caused by disgust. She recognized desire, and knew she had to stop this, now, before she disgraced herself. She turned her face toward him. "Stop! You've no right." Her voice was breathless.

"You don't really want me to stop." He smiled, a confident, wicked smile that told her he knew only too well how to interpret her response. "Come, give me my kiss, my dear, and let us cry friends."

"I'd rather be horsewhipped," she snapped. She felt him catch his breath, and looked up into the chocolate depths of his eyes. She was a liar, and knew it. She was trembling for his kiss. But she faced him down, her glare unwavering.

His smile faded. Pulling away from her, he thrust her from the door, exiting on a muttered, "Take care I don't oblige you!" He turned just before she slammed it, and placing his foot to prevent her, admonished, "Mind—notify me when Miss Allen replies. No delay or you'll be very sorry."

Gwynneth locked the door behind him until she could restore her hair—and her mind—to some semblance of order.

Trembling, she fumbled with hairpins while wishing she had never begun the correspondence with that vile man. How could she have thought him sensitive? Kind? Caring? The person he had seemed in his letters was unreal, she now realized, a literary fiction created by himself for some unknown purpose.

The view the world had of him was the true one after all—a hard, arrogant, unprincipled rake. She recalled her father's gentle admonition when she had told him how different Lord Langley seemed in his letters from what she read of him in the newspapers. "I expect in his letters he takes his cue from his correspondents, presenting the side of himself most agreeable to each. Like the chameleon, he colors himself to his own advantage."

She opened the little chest, took up his letter, and looked at it miserably. She would not open it. She knew now what a monster he was. No more would she correspond with him.

Sadly she consigned the unopened letter to the dustbin. It cost her a pang to bury the epistolary Lord Langley, but any pleasure she had taken in their correspondence was ended by this bruising contact with the real thing.

Chapter Two

As Stuart Hamilton, Baron Langley, rode back to Nicholas Verleigh's house party, he was seething with anger. He was angry with his longtime correspondent, Miss Allen, for refusing to reveal her identity to him; angry with Miss Dunlevvy for refusing to cooperate in helping him to locate Miss Allen; and most of all angry, in fact furious, with himself for behaving in so unforgivable a manner to the young bookseller.

As he slowed his big bay gelding, Turk, to a canter on the Verleigh grounds, he wondered what had caused him to be so aggressive toward Miss Dunlevvy. Something about the girl's coolness, her self-assured manner, had set him off. Just a shopkeeper's daughter, after all, though with a surprisingly cultured voice. It was her self-possessed, almost superior manner, that had annoyed him. Still, he couldn't excuse himself. "That was badly done, Stuart," he muttered.

The fact that he had behaved so abominably as to force his attentions on any woman, much less a shopkeeper, was bad enough, but that he should choose *this* shopkeeper! He desperately needed to turn her up sweet, not alienate her. She was his only link to Miss Allen.

Not that he wanted to alienate her, in any case. He felt a tug of desire as he recalled her soft curves pressed against him. Stop that, Stuart, he lectured himself. The pretty little bookseller wasn't what he had come to Guilford for, and any involvement with her would no doubt quite sink him with Miss Allen. As it was, this day's ill-advised amorousness would get back to his correspondent, increasing her reluctance to meet him.

Stuart's self-deprecating musings ended as a footman came running forward to take his rangy bay's head as he drew up in front of the Verleigh mansion. He had always felt that the massive new Georgian mansion was in strange contrast to its setting here in the romantic Lake Country, near Lake Windemere. Its strict, classic proportions and tidy formal grounds would have been more at home, it seemed to Stuart, on a flat, open Yorkshire landscape. But Nicholas's father, who had made a fortune in real estate as London expanded into the surrounding countryside, had determinedly set up a modern, elegant, classically proportioned country home in the midst of one of the most scenic and rustic areas of England.

As his long legs carried him up the stairs, Langley's mind was not on architecture, however, but on his morning's faux pas. He promised himself he would make amends to this Miss Dunlevvy. "Dunlevvy . . . Dunlevvy . . . An aristocratic name for a shopkeeper," he muttered through clinched teeth.

"So, Stu, it has come to this! Talking to yourself, dear boy!" The genial tones of his host, Nicholas Verleigh, arrested his stride as he turned down the hall to his rooms to change clothes. "What's this about Miss Dunlevvy?"

Stuart sighed and turned around. Nicholas was a favorite of his, but the short, slightly chubby blond was alert and inquisitive to a fault. To get information from him without giving out twice as much in return was a true challenge!

"The bookseller, Miss Dunlevvy, you know her? Well-spoken and with a proud, almost haughty manner—and that aristocratic name. Strikes me as odd in a gel who's in trade, after all."

"Been out so early to buy books? You never can get

enough, can you? But did you not check my library? Perhaps I have what you want?"

When Stuart didn't respond, Nicholas continued. "But I take it Miss Dunlevvy put a bee in your bonnet to send you away empty-handed and talking to yourself, too."

"Thrust my blunt back in my hand when I attempted to pay her for a trifling service." He lashed his boots with his whip at the memory.

"The insipid, oh-so-genteel Miss Dunlevvy? Odds Bodkins! But how did she come to be accepting your money? She never clerks."

"I've no idea," Langley snapped. "Why shouldn't she clerk, though. Owns a bookstore, don't she?"

"Though a mere bookseller now, she seldom forgets she's an earl's granddaughter." Nicholas grinned at the obvious astonishment on his friend's face.

"An earl's granddaughter. Then what is she doing tending a shop?"

"Her father had a falling out with his family because of his strange democratical notions. Called him a Jacobin, a charge you are all too familiar with." At Langley's nod, Verleigh continued. "Why he chose to open a bookstore, I don't know, but Miss Dunlevvy inherited the business from him."

"And his Jacobin ideas, too?" Langley's interest was ever more piqued.

"As to that, I couldn't say. Miss Dunlevvy keeps her own counsel."

"That I can believe. Rudest chit it has been my misfortune to meet in a while," Langley growled, turning into his room and unceremoniously shutting the door in Nicholas's face.

He left his host frowning in puzzlement. He was most dissatisfied by the conversation, which left him not knowing what his friend had been doing at a bookshop so early on his first day in attendance at their summer house party.

Why was Miss Dunlevvy clerking? Why was she so rude to Stuart? And why was Stuart so out of reason cross with her? He wandered downstairs, enjoying the perplexity that kept boredom at bay. This must be gotten to the bottom of!

That evening a weary Gwynneth mounted the stairs that led to the rooms over her shop. Her clerk, Mr. Ezekial Highley, had gone to Kendal that day to visit his sick mother, and she had been forced to keep the shop open herself. She disliked doing so, but late in the day there had been several customers, so she was glad that she had not closed her doors. How desperately every bit of business was needed if her plan were to succeed!

She carried with her Lord Langley's letter, which she had retrieved from the dustbin. All day long she had been aware of it lying there, gradually being buried under other trash, but burning its way into her consciousness. When she had locked the door after the last customer, she had tried to walk past it without retrieving it, but it seemed to exert a siren-like pull on her, and now she stood in the golden circle of the oil lamp by her parlor table, turning it over in her hand.

She made up her mind not to read it until Lord Langley had left Guilford. Once he was in London again, she could decide whether to reply or not. She did not want to risk reading it. In spite of his behavior today, his eloquent letter writing might convince her against her will to make herself known to him.

With a sigh, she placed it on the top of a packet of similar letters and started to return them to their repository in the locked drawer of a massive desk, one of several pieces of good furniture she had been able to bring with her from the vicarage when her father had left the ministry.

On an impulse she withdrew them and turned the packet over, extracting her copy of the first letter she had ever written to him, and his response.

My Dear Lord Langley:

You will perhaps be more inclined to forgive this uninvited intrusion when you learn that it is with the purpose of supporting your plan for a magazine devoted to the literary productions of women.

You asserted in the *Review* that there were numerous able women writers in our country, but that many of them were too modest, too closely supervised, or too inhibited to place their work before the curious eyes of the reading public.

I agree with you that these are all excellent explanations for women's reticence to publish. But you yourself were far too modest about the good your proposed magazine could do when you failed to include perhaps my sex's biggest hindrance in literary affairs—the lack of encouragement.

There are far too many of your sex who inveigh against "women scribblers," ridiculing the very idea of a woman having thoughts worth sharing, much less the ability to clothe them in appealing literary dress. Women can seldom find space in magazines crowded with the productions of men, nor, I believe, are their submissions judged objectively.

I will intrude on you no farther than to submit a small poem of my own, "Lines on the End of a Summer Day." I do not pretend this shall rise to the heights of Shakespeare, the emotional coloring of Moore, or the cleverness of Byron. In truth, I do not know if it has any excellencies at all, for another thing women seldom receive is dispassionate criticism aimed at helping them improve rather than ridiculing or patronizing them.

Whether or not you find this poem worthy of its pages, I will eagerly look forward to the publication of *The Legacy*, your new magazine devoted to the works of women authors.

Thank you for your time and attention, and believe me your humble and admiring servant,

Miss Suzanne Allen

P.S. If your lordship should by any rare chance wish to communicate with me, you may do so through M. Dunlevvy, Bookseller, Guilford.

The reply was not long in arriving. Lord Langley's hasty and difficult-to-read handwriting caused her much trouble at first to decipher. She still remembered how astonished she had been by its breezy informality and almost total lack of punctuation.

Dear Miss Allen—
    Yr "Lines on the End etc. I find quite charming will you permit me one stricture you did say you'd welcome dispassionate criticism—the line ending "dainty dews" is obviously meant to echo the "deepening hues" in the first stanza A tri-syllabic word would intensify this effect—delicate perhaps?
    Other than that, it is a very pretty production, and I ask leave to include it in our first issue We are offering a very modest fee to our new authors which I hope you will accept tho I know you are a gentlewoman it is herewith enclosed—Please favor me with more examples of yr work—

                                                        Langley

P.S. By yr choice and treatment of subject matter I conclude you are young and on principle you must be pretty therefore will you send me yr direction that I may seek you out and make love to you—no more than you like—mind—and very discreetly if you be married.

                                                        L.

This reply had brought much soul-searching. How happy his praise had made her, but the flirtatious, highly improper postscript almost kept her from replying. At last she had written:

Dear Lord Langley:
    Please accept my humble thanks for your kind words about "Lines on the End of a Summer Day." I can never reveal my direction to you, nor my true name, and am most reluctant to communicate further if subjected to the kind of gallantries contained in your postscript, even upon paper. You wrote in the preface to "Gravemont in New England"

that "all women expect all men to make love to them, and a kind man lives up to their expectations, however slight the token he offers."

I assure you I do *not* expect it and cannot countenance any further such hints.

I enclose a short essay on a country character, in hopes it will interest you. I remain, etc., etc.,

Miss Suzanne Allen

Though she knew it almost by heart, Gwynneth lifted his next letter out of the pile and reread it, smiling in spite of herself.

Dear Miss Allen—

You are severe with me and yet yr new essay is not that of a woman either unforgiving or hard of heart—indeed you must be . . . I had almost written down a Greek epigram but if you know Greek you would have blushed and withdrawn from our correspondence, and if you do not it would be pointless and pedantic in me to so address you so I will content myself with another quote from Gravemont "She was demure and proper and discreet" and therefore I will say no more now don't be a naughty puss and look up the next line, for you might then think I've broken yr strict commandment and am flirting with you I assure you I am not—I am—until you wish otherwise—yr sober solemn editor and as such beg more jewels like these last you have sent me for I have been inundated by submissions for *The Legacy* but precious little of it deserves the name of literature—

Believe me yr etc etc

L

The next line of his famous poem was known to her, of course, as he had surely guessed it would be. A smile quirked her mouth as she folded the letter and whispered it:

"And her love was fiery and her kisses sweet."

He was, in his letters, an engaging rogue. She blushed to think how much she had wished to read his Greek epigram!

Thus had begun a literary correspondence that had come to mean more and more to Gwynneth, buried as she was in country obscurity and isolation following her father's sinking into trade. A place in society was lost to her. The intellectual life that she was so well fitted to enjoy was denied her except through these letters.

They came to represent to her a hope of escape from her dull life, not merely for the growing pile of coins she saved as her father cashed Langley's payments for her writings. Far more important than the money she had earned thus far, was the hope it gave her that she would be able to earn more someday, through her writing—perhaps enough that she might leave Guilford, with its closed society, and live independently in the great city of London, able to sample its vast wares of concerts, lectures, art exhibits, and, most importantly, intellectual companions.

She had learned to fend off Lord Langley's attempts at flirtation, his exhortations to reveal her direction so he could visit her, with arch humor. Yet she secretly treasured these provocative sallies, which often approached the lover-like in tone, especially lately. "My dearest blue," he had recently written, "you are the sweetest blue and the bluest blue of all the bluestocking crowd. If you would only appear before me I wd show you how I have learnt to worship that color by so many men abhorred."

She had felt a growing sense of closeness to the sensitive Lord Langley as he confided his thoughts to her with ever deepening intimacy.

No more. No more. The reality had turned out to be a man who was crude, boorish, temperamental, and completely callous to a woman's feelings, taking pleasure from and offering insult to helpless females on the least pretext.

Perhaps soon she would be able to sell the bookshop and go to London, thus achieving her secret, long-cherished goal. Perhaps when she arrived there she might emulate some of the other "blue" ladies and earn her bread with her pen.

Until then, however, she was now cut off from intellectual society as truly as she was from the social life of this little corner of England. And cut off from the friendship with Lord Langley, which she had begun to treasure so deeply.

Gwynneth dashed a tear from her eye and urged herself not to repine as she bundled the letters back into their locked drawer. If only she could somehow put her feelings as firmly under lock and key.

Chapter Three

Lord Langley dressed hurriedly that evening, eager to join his friends below, where he hoped Nicholas had invited some of the local gentry to join their house party. Perhaps "Miss Allen" would be among them. Perhaps she would decide to step out from behind her nom de plume, or if not, perhaps he could discover her from something she said.

He virtually bounded down the stairs and into the grand salon, where the small number gathered led him to believe he had arrived early. His hopes that more would be joining them were dashed when Nicholas greeted him with, "Ah, Stuart, now we are all here."

Still, he optimistically allowed himself to be introduced to those few he didn't know. Lady Trumbull, her daughter Elizabeth, and Lady Trumbull's niece Constance Blackwood were first presented to him.

"You live near Guilford, Lady Elizabeth?" he queried hopefully.

"No, Lord Langley, we are from Yorkshire. This is our first visit to the Lake Country."

"So picturesque! So poetic." Lady Trumbull nodded her turbaned head vigorously, causing the several tall plumes that adorned it to bob alarmingly. "I can quite see why you poets love it. Doubtless we shall see something from your pen to commemorate this occasion?"

Suppressing a shudder, Langley murmured something inconsequential and turned his attention to the niece, a dark-haired pocket Venus who stood by her aunt looking every which way in obvious embarrassment over her effusiveness.

"And you, Miss Blackwood? Are you Nicholas's neighbor, by any chance?"

Her eyes twinkled mischievously. "I, too, am seeing Wordsworth's beloved land of daffodils and waterfalls for the first time." Delightful dimples appeared at her smile. "I have to confess I like the country much better than his poetry."

"I wonder you came here during the victory celebrations. Perhaps you share with our host and myself a disgust of the restoration of the Bourbons?"

Miss Blackwood wrinkled her nose disdainfully. "It is too bad, isn't it. Just because we have defeated Napoleon, it doesn't mean that we should destroy his many excellent reforms, or . . . "

"Now, Constance, you have been listening too much to Lord Dudley. Such talk borders on the disloyal, and I won't have it! Why, your father would be horrified."

"Yes, Aunt," the petite brunette responded meekly, but flashed Langley a look that said she held fast to her opinions.

Lord Langley's eyes roamed the room restively. If these women were not natives of the Lake Country, none of them could possibly be his "Miss Allen," as both her poems and essays were inextricably linked to this very special place. Searching for another possibility, he espied a lovely blond matron speaking with John McDougal and Roger, Earl of Dudley.

"Excuse me a moment, ladies, but I must greet some friends." He extricated himself firmly from the little group and approached the young earl, clapping him on the shoulders and claiming an introduction to his lovely companion.

Roger somewhat reluctantly presented him to the plumply pretty woman at his side, Lady Alana Morley.

"Lord Dudley has been teasing me, sir, that he might abdicate his title. I cannot believe that he would do such a thing, or that you would encourage him."

"Lud, ma'am, certainly not. Roger, what start is this?"

John McDougal chuckled softly. "I've tried to assure the cub that you don't mean him to abdicate."

"B-but you wrote so convincingly in the *Quarterly Review* against inherited honors. I thought . . . " Dudley turned confused eyes on the man he aspired to emulate.

Completely forgetting his interest in the blonde for a moment, Langley gave his young disciple a savage look. "You foolish young whelp. What good would it do to give up our titles if the Tory lords don't? Think, man! They'd be even more powerful than they are now. We can't take on society one at a time. Now the war is over, we'll need every vote we can get in the House of Lords, if we are ever to achieve meaningful reform. Then would be time to vote to suspend titles."

"La, as if you ever would!" Lady Morley dimpled at the two. "I vow you are both quizzing me. At any rate, I hope so."

"By no means, madam, assure you I am not. But Roger, you must remain earl and take your seat in Lords this next Parliament. Your hand on it."

"Indeed I shall, sir. Now I understand you." Red-faced, the younger man shook hands deferentially with his mentor.

"Why would you wish to see abolished a system which has served us well for so long?" Lady Morley frowned in perplexity.

"It has served us, perhaps, but has it served those who don't have titles?"

"But isn't that one of the strengths of our system, that those who achieve, who show superior contributions to our society, can hope one day to earn a title?"

Young Dudley strove to regain the fetching matron's attention, now challengingly centered on Langley. "We don't object to recognizing accomplishments, Lady Morley, only to passing the honors on in perpetuity to offspring who may be perfectly undistinguished."

"Well, I see I must not dispute with two such formidable opponents, or I shall have the headache. Do let us talk of something other than politics." She gave a pretty pout. Dudley eagerly took up her suggestion, and while they flirted, Langley appraised the blond matron through hooded eyes. A little above his age, though well short of forty, she was curvaceous and stylish. Her blond hair was beautifully dressed `a la greque.

It is possible, just possible, he thought. She argued on the wrong side on titles, one of the areas in which he and "Miss Allen" were in perfect agreement. But the woman had wit and intellect, clearly. Mightn't "Miss Allen" take positions different from the opinions in her letters to throw dust in his eyes?

His opportunity to learn more about Lady Morley was postponed as dinner was announced. He was placed between Lady Trumbull and her daughter Elizabeth. Lady Elizabeth, spent most of her time chatting with John McDougal on her other side, and Lady Trumbull alternately bored and infuriated him with her loudly voiced political opinions.

He chafed at the delay as the men lingered over port, and was prepared to abandon them for the ladies when something was said in jest to Sir Alfred Morley about being at Nicholas's house party instead of roistering with Prinny and his friends in London.

Not quite understanding the gist of the conversation, to which he had bent but half an ear, Langley queried, "You're not here like John and Roger and I to seek refuge from the self-congratulatory madness in London, then?"

"Pon rep, no. Love to be there. Thought my lady would

leave me for her lover when I said we'd come here instead of staying in London. Woman abominates the country." He chuckled as if wearing a cuckold's horns was a good joke.

"But I'd need of a repairing lease, don't you see. Badly dipped. Dibs not in tune. Grateful Lady Trumbull asked for my escort here, don't you know. I'll toddle off to my estate in Hertford in a few weeks, try being a country gentleman for a while."

Langley had little interest in Sir Alfred's financial problems, but as he examined this speech he found considerable doubt cast on his hopes that Lady Morley might be his "Miss Allen."

For his elusive poetess clearly loved the country, and now that he thought of it, had written that she had never been to London.

Then, too, the letters revealed a morally strict, even prim, woman, hardly the sort to have a lover, even secretly, much less so openly that her complaisant husband joked of it.

The seal was set on his conclusion during his conversation with Lady Morley when they joined the ladies in the drawing room.

He went straight to her side, and was amused at the way she preened at this sign of interest. Clearly she was not mourning her lost lover overmuch. He glanced at her husband, who had quickly joined Lady Trumbull.

"Sir Alfred indicates you do not like to rusticate, Lady Morley."

"Please, call me Alana." She laid one white dimpled hand on his sleeve. "At such a small gathering surely we can be more informal."

A self-deprecatory grin lit his dark eyes. "I could hardly argue against abolishing titles at one house party, when I advocate abolishing them altogether."

"Well, then, in answer to your question, Stuart, I do dread this impending period of rustification, which Alfred insists is absolutely necessary. I've spent my entire life avoiding the country, and have been largely successful until now."

"Then this is your first visit to the Lake Country. Shall you make a pilgrimmage to visit Wordsworth?" He hardly needed her answer to draw his conclusions.

She wrinkled her slightly retroussé nose. "I can't care for his poetry, full of daffodils and clouds. I much prefer the more manly poetry of Byron's "Childe Harold" or your own "Gravemont.""

He bowed to her in acknowledgment of the compliment. "Of course your own poetry has nothing of daffodils or clouds in it, I expect?" He watched her features for any betraying consciousness but saw none as she laughed gaily.

"La, me write poetry, sir? Do I look a bluestocking? My talents lie rather in appreciation, I believe." Here she took his arm and leaned toward him in a rather provocative manner. "I do so appreciate a manly poet!"

A sardonic grin twisted his lips. With the emphasis on the adjective, he thought. Giving up all notion that this forward baggage could be his elusive poetess, he determinedly changed the subject, inducing her to give him a song or two. She permitted herself to be led to the piano, where she settled herself charmingly and began a very competent rendition of a Clementi sonata.

Langley withdrew to the balcony to blow a cloud and contemplate his lack of success. None of the women he'd met tonight could be his "Miss Allen." As he brooded over his next move, his reverie was interrupted by a Scots brogue in his ear.

"Does it nae strike ye that this is a curst odd assortment of a house party?" John McDougal made no attempt to smooth his accent for his longtime friend.

"Aye, it does and all." Langley grinned, echoing his friend's accent teasingly. "What can have been in Nicholas's mind, I wonder, inviting the Trumbulls and the Morleys? When this house party was proposed, it was to be for those of us who wished to escape the victory celebrations in London."

" 'Tis easily answered, though you'll no like it. 'Twas the only way he could get Miss Blackwood to come."

"Umph! Serious matter, courting an unmarried miss!"

"I believe he is quite serious about it."

Silence descended on the two friends as Langley contemplated the implications of this. At last he growled, "That explains the Trumbulls, but . . . "

"And Lady Trumbull's *cher ami* is Sir Alfred Morley, who coincidentally must escape the duns. Nicholas's house party was most opportune, though I believe the deluded aunt hopes her niece will fix Roger's interest instead of Nicholas's."

"Prefers a title to a fortune, does she?"

"Aye. For Miss Constance has a fortune of her own, d'ye ken."

"Then she'd be well-advised to remain unwed!"

John chuckled. "I'd a notion you'd say that. But I doubt either she or Nicholas would agree." He motioned toward the piano in the drawing room. Several members of the house party had gathered around to sing to Lady Morley's accompaniment. Nicholas and Constance, taking advantage of the need to share a sheet of music, were standing shoulder to shoulder.

"It's pleased I am that the Trumbulls were invited, any road. 'Tis giving me the chance to spend some time with Lady Elizabeth. A braw lassie she is, no mistake."

"Not you, too, John."

"Fear not, lad. She's a dutiful daughter, and Lady Trumbull would never let her think on the likes of a radical like me."

Young Dudley's slightly off-key tenor brought a frown to McDougal's brows. "I say, Stu, a bit hard on Roger earlier this evening, weren't you."

Langley shook his head regretfully. "I was indeed! I'll

apologize to him handsomely, I swear. You know I've the devil's own temper at times." He laughed ruefully, and then growled in a low, contemptuous tone, "Like my father, unfortunately."

"Aye, but unlike your father, you regret giving rein to it, often as not." McDougal thumped his friend on the back in a masculine gesture of comfort.

As the two friends watched, something distracted the group around the piano, and Nicholas detached himself to go toward the entry door, where a man was walking into the drawing room as if he owned it.

"Devil-a-bit! Isn't that Barlow?"

Lord Langley stepped forward for a better look. "Damned if it isn't! Sir Miles Barlow, here! What on earth for?" They watched as their old acquaintance and enemy was being introduced to the other guests. His dark auburn hair and long, thin auburn mustachios were styled to further his oft-remarked resemblance to Lord Byron. He was handsome in a rather dandified way, and very polished in society, but both men regarded him with disgust, knowing from school days that his smooth manners hid a vicious disposition.

"We'd best go in and lend Nicholas moral support." McDougal started toward the open windows.

"I'd rather throw him in his own fishpond for inviting that bit of slime here."

"A monkey says he wasn't invited."

"No, I don't think I'll take that bet. You're likely right. Nicholas would never invite Barlow to a house party."

It didn't take long to confirm that Sir Miles had just "happened to be in the area" and had come to pay his respects. He was staying at the White Hart, Guilford's one decent hostelry.

"What brings you to this picturesque corner of England, Miles? Most unlike you to rusticate at such a time." Langley was glad to hear the insatiably curious Nicholas asking the question.

"Oh, just looking into a little matter for HRH. As you are surely aware, I am working for the government now. We may have defeated the French, but we still have enemies here at home, as well you know."

Sir Miles slanted an insinuating look at Langley from beneath heavy eyelids. "And how surprising to see two of our peers of the realm here when all of England is in London helping entertain our distinguished visitors and celebrate the peace."

"Celebrate the reinstatement of that fat Bourbon slug Louis, you mean! Never!" The excitable Lord Dudley looked as if he might attack Barlow for the suggestion.

"If all of England is in London, then shouldn't you be there too, Miles? Have you thought of all the free food and liquor you're missing?" Langley looked down his nose dismissively at the overdressed and overgroomed man before him.

"A small matter of a seditious newspaper to shut down. Shouldn't take a week. Though I'll admit *your* presence here makes me question whether the matter is as simple as I'd first thought. At any rate, I'll soon be back in London, ready to do my duty by the Prince Regent. Lady Trumbull—surprised to see you in this hotbed of radicalism."

"Nothing to do with politics, young man. Anyone knows I'm a staunch Tory. But my niece, Miss Blackwood, always becomes quite ill if she stays in London when it begins to get hot. The miasmas, you know. So we were pleased to receive Mr. Verleigh's invitation . . . "

"Indeed, ma'am." Barlow firmly stemmed her flow of words. "And will you present me to the charming young lady?"

As they watched Barlow try to ingratiate himself with the petite heiress, Langley asked his friend, "Is there a liberal newspaper in Guilford, Nick?"

"There was. Martin Dunlevvy had a very fine paper, actually more a journal of opinion."

"Miss Dunlevvy's father, the bookseller?"

"The same. He also owned a small print shop, and among other things printed his and others' opinions, usually in opposition to the government. But he was always careful not to step over the line. This charge of sedition is ridiculous."

"That line seems to move around quite a bit, as our Tory government becomes more entrenched in its power and more repressive. Certainly the Hunts were taken by surprise by its serpentine twists." The young men solemnly contemplated their good friends the Hunt brothers, who were awaiting trial for having printed material objectionable to the government.

Barlow must have been keeping one ear cocked toward their conversation. "So you know of Mr. Dunlevvy's rag, eh, Nick? It occurs to me you may even have contributed to it. I've always suspected you gentlemen's journalistic activities were going to place you in danger sooner or later." He slanted an insinuating look at the four men.

"I defy anyone to find anything disloyal in anything I have ever written. Sometimes the most loyal act is that of constructive criticism." Langley's brown eyes flashed with fury.

"Well, I am sure I hope you are right, Stuart. But unfortunately for Mr. Dunlevvy, he cannot say the same. His rag is full of the grossest libels and seditious statements, not to mention every kind of vulgarity. Intend to arrest him tomorrow."

Barlow was visibly annoyed when Langley and Verleigh both broke into laughter at this assertion. "You think it is funny? You'll be laughing out of the other side of your faces soon. And I intend to track down all who had anything to do with this venture, too." All four friends were encompassed in his angry glare.

"I don't put it past this government to dig a dead man up, try him, and hang him, Miles. So kind of them to keep the

cages along our highways so charmingly decorated."
Nicholas rocked back on his heels, laughing silently. "But
you will find it very difficult in Dunlevvy's case, as he was
cremated six months ago."

"Cremated? Pagan, that's what it is, pagan." Lady Trumbull's head nodded until her turban almost fell off. "And to
think that he was an ordained priest in the Church of England. The scandal!"

"Dead these six months," Barlow drawled thoughtfully.
"How very interesting." He took the news unexpectedly
well, seeming almost pleased by it. Langley's heavy eyebrows shot up as he watched the dandy turn his attention to
the women.

"Ah, Lady Morley. I recall hearing you sing enchant-
ingly at a musicale at Lady Sefton's last season. I don't
suppose you would be kind enough to indulge me?"

Barlow took Alana's dimpled elbow and led her toward
the piano, leaving Langley to shrug at the perplexity in his
friends' eyes.

It was quite late when Sir Miles took his leave and the
house party broke up for the night, so Langley did not have
a chance to discuss with Nicholas his premonition that they
had not heard the last charge of sedition from their old
schoolmate.

Chapter Four

Lord Langley knew he must repair his fences with the comely young bookseller. Miss Dunlevvy had spoken as if she merely forwarded the letters to Miss Allen, yet her tenacity in refusing information suggested a personal knowledge of her correspondent and an interest in preserving her privacy.

Also, he truly felt repentant of his rash act. Something about the self-possessed manner of Miss Dunlevvy had tormented him in much the same way as Miss Allen's witty but firm refusals to comply with his wishes for a meeting. He realized that some of his frustration at being unable to locate his elusive correspondent had erupted in his cavalier treatment of Miss Dunlevvy.

He would have to humble himself, to ingratiate himself with her and convince her he was not a despicable rogue, though he himself was not entirely convinced. His complex nature was a puzzle and a worry, even to himself, and he had gotten into many scrapes and earned a most unenviable reputation in the *ton* as a result. He really did not consider himself a rake, for example, though he had that reputation. The hapless young bookseller doubtless now thought his reputation well deserved.

To begin repairing his fences with Miss Dunlevvy, he organized an expedition into the village the next day, taking along Nicholas, Roger, John, Miss Constance Blackwood,

Lady Alana Morley, Lady Elizabeth Trumbull, and her mother.

The latter went along most reluctantly, as the shops of the provincial village could not, she felt, have anything to interest her. Only her determination to see Miss Blackwood riveted to Lord Dudley caused her to overcome her disdain. Her niece never put herself forward with him, so she must needs push them together whenever possible.

Lady Trumbull was particularly cutting when she learned Lord Langley meant to visit M. Dunlevvy's bookshop. "That radical sympathizer, that Jacobin traitor . . . why he wasn't whipped at the carttail and run out of this county I'll never know!" She cast indignant glances about her, seeking confirmation of her opinion.

"But the old man is dead and in the ground," Nicholas protested. "Likely Miss Dunlevvy's politics are as dull as her personality."

Langley raised his eyebrows in surprise at this comment. He had thought the fetching young bookseller somewhat of a firebrand, personally. But as he did not wish to explain why, he only observed that he liked to prowl around provincial bookshops; rare first editions could occasionally be found in such out-of-the-way places.

"She is very likely a secret Jacobin like her father. The fruit doesn't fall far from the tree," Lady Trumbull sniffed. "That she would continue operating that shop after his death shows that."

The baron, riding beside the open carriage which held the ladies, winked across at Nicholas, riding opposite. "Yes, I've heard bookselling makes one a Jacobin. I suppose it is inevitable that John Murray will one day reveal his true colors." He chuckled at the thought of the conservative London bookseller and publisher being unmasked as a revolutionary.

"If truth were told, you're likely no better, considering

all those *déclassé* personages you hang about with." Lady Trumbull sniffed and turned her head away.

"There's a facer for you, Langley! S'a wonder you've not been thrown into jail for a traitor by now." Roger brayed his amusement at Lady Trumbull's censorious opinion.

Langley laughed and turned his attention to Lady Morley. "Will you come and visit me in prison, Alana, and cheer my dark cell with your beauty?"

Lady Morley tilted her small, shapely head up and looked from under her fashionable chip-straw bonnet at him with laughing blue eyes. "You may count on me, my lord. Especially if you shall furnish your cell charmingly. Between you and the Hunts, visiting prisoners shall doubtless become the *dernier cri!*"

"I shall even provide you with a piano, so you may beguile my lonely hours." Stuart's eyes held an approving gleam as he saluted Lady Morley. In point of fact, Alana had made it clear that he could count on her for a great deal. The shapely matron was certainly a temptation, and her husband was too occupied with his current mistress to care whom his wife entertained in her bed. Though how the man could prefer Lady Trumbull to the buxom blonde defied imagination. Nevertheless, Alana was obviously both free and eager to choose a lover.

To his surprise, Stuart felt no real temptation to bed her. Nor was it likely that his purpose in coming to Guilford would be furthered by beginning an illicit affair, so he would have to take care not to give the lovely lady much encouragement.

The bookstore occupied a fine freestanding two-story stone building near the center of the small market town. On either side were various small but apparently prosperous businesses, including a haberdasher, a modiste, and a sweetshop. When their entourage pulled up in front of Dunlevvy's, they immediately lost the female contingent to the modiste and the sweetshop. Roger accompanied the ladies, leaving Nicholas and John to enter the bookshop with Stuart.

Glad that the ladies would not be conning his next encounter with Miss Dunlevvy, Langley paused inside to give his eyes time to adjust to the darkness after the bright sunshine. Soon he made out two customers at a reading table, and a clerk behind the counter, wrapping a packet of books for another. Miss Dunlevvy was nowhere in sight.

"Told you she don't clerk. Must have been somethin' wrong with old Highley there, for you to find her in the shop." Nicholas sounded smug.

Langley walked directly to the counter and addressed the tall, thin, middle-aged clerk imperiously. "I'd like to see Miss Dunlevvy, please."

"If I may be of service, sir? She is not available."

"No, my business is with Miss Dunlevvy. When do you expect her?"

Mr. Highley looked uncomfortable. Chewing on his gray, drooping mustache, he considered his options. To deny anything to such an obviously high-in-the-instep gentleman made him very nervous, but Miss Dunlevvy had been working on the accounts all morning and had asked not to be disturbed. It always made Miss Dunlevvy cross to work on the accounts.

At that moment the rest of the Verleigh party burst into the room, chattering about the sweetshop next door. "Do come see, Stuart, the adorable biscuits we found in the shape of soldiers, decorated in proper regimentals and everything."

Langley stepped over to look at Lady Morley's purchase, and Highley took this opportunity to slip into the back. "Miss Dunlevvy, the shop is full of quality, and one of the gents is demanding to see you."

Gwynneth looked up, frowning, then stood and stretched. Her heart gave a little skip. Was it Langley?

She peered around the door to see him holding something small, his dark head bowed near the golden curls and fetching flower-trimmèd bonnet of a very well-dressed, attractive young matron. They were laughing.

Gwynneth felt a surprising rush of awareness as she saw the tall form of Lord Langley in her shop once more. Mercy! Why did she feel such excitement? The man was odious. And why did she feel a twist of jealousy at the way he was smiling at the buxom blonde?

She scanned the rest of the shop; seldom was it so full. She recognized Nicholas Verleigh, a frequent customer and occasional contributor to her father's newspaper, and Lady Trumbull, who had never been in the establishment before. She knew the lady from long ago, when she had visited Gwynneth's grandfather, the earl.

She realized she'd have to be civil to Langley. She needed the custom of every educated person in the community if she was to build up her business. Her father had driven most of the gentry away with his radical notions, but she needed an improved custom if she was to sell the bookstore at a decent price. This did her conscience no violence, for she had not agreed with her father on a great many things, and felt no crusading zeal to antagonize the gentry.

Nipping back into her office to check her reflection in a mirror, she reassured herself that her hair was still firmly contained in its braids, and that no ink had found its way to her face. She then emerged from the back of the shop and approached Lord Langley with a calmness she didn't feel.

"You wished to speak to me, my lord?"

Stuart turned from Lady Morley and surveyed his erstwhile antagonist. She was dressed in black again, a most unbecoming color on her, and her wheaten hair was brutally contained in tight braids. Her self-possessed face looked up at him quite as if their contretemps had never taken place.

He suppressed a surge of irritable desire to blast her

composure to shreds, and flashed what he hoped was an ingratiating smile at her. "Yes. Might I have a word in private?"

To Gwynneth it looked a devilish smile, full of self-confidence, but she nodded calmly and led him to her office. There she turned, her round golden-hazel eyes wide with concern.

"I feel that I must . . . "

"Honesty compels me . . . "

They both rushed into speech at the same time, then stopped, somewhat flustered.

"The other day when I . . . "

"It was certainly not my intention . . . "

This time Gwynneth giggled, and Stuart shook his head in self-mockery. "Go ahead, Miss Dunlevvy."

"Thank you, my lord. I have been thinking upon my behavior the other day, and I realize that I *was* rather impertinent. Though I must object strongly to your reaction, I do accept my share of the blame. I beg you will forgive me."

Langley looked astonished. "*I* forgive *you*? But what I did was inexcusable. I can't really say what it was got into me, unless . . . " He tilted his head, giving her a flirtatious look that did strange things to Gwynneth's breathing. "Unless it was the adorable way your mouth tips up at the corners. Or perhaps that enchanting trail of angel dust across your nose?"

It was Gwynneth's turn to look astonished. She pursed her lips and put her hands on her hips. "I am persuaded there was more of anger than admiration in your behavior."

Stuart sighed and admitted disarmingly, "It is true, I suppose. I never did take no for an answer easily, especially from a woman I'd much rather would say yes to me."

Now Gwynneth laughed aloud. "You are a scamp, and if you think I'll swallow all this . . . this fustian, you are much mistaken."

His dark eyes crinkled with amusement as he moved

closer, taking her hand. "No, I don't suppose you will, but at least I've made you laugh. I do apologize for my behavior. May we cry friends, my dear?"

As she had yesterday, Gwynneth once again had that peculiar feeling of drowning as she gazed into the chocolate depths of his eyes. She drew her hand away and stepped back. "Yes, friends." Then, to turn his thoughts and hers in another direction, she volunteered, "Miss Allen hasn't yet replied to your note."

Her diversion was instantly successful. "You have sent it to her then? Excellent!" Then, thoughtfully, "She must live very near if you might have received a reply by now."

Gwynneth swallowed hard. Lying was so difficult. "It was handled in the usual way" was her ambiguous response.

He stood with his head bowed, looking so forlorn that Gwynneth was hard put to keep up her pretence. To comfort him she offered, "I'll let you know right away when a letter comes." Then she bit her lip in self-annoyance. She had meant not to reply at all—not even to read his note, for that matter. She had intended to break off the correspondence. What was she doing promising him another letter?

Langley lifted his head and gave her a dazzling smile. "Thank you. And I promise not to insult you by pressing a guinea on you." He turned toward the door of her office. "Instead, I'll look over your stock. I am sure a bibliophile like me can find something worthy of purchase here."

She inclined her head. "We are not perhaps so well stocked as your London bookshops, but it was ever my father's pride to be current with the latest publications."

She dropped to her chair after he gave her a little bow and returned to his companions in the shop. A fine trembling had for some reason seized her body. Oh, he was a *very* dangerous man. He had her eating out of his hands, he who had behaved so despicably the last time he was here!

How could such a tall, powerfully built, arrogant man have managed to look so little-boy wistful?

What could she say in a letter to discourage him as she must? He was irrepressible and well-nigh irresistible!

Langley watched approvingly as the ladies, in spite of Lady Trumbull's strictures, purchased a selection of novels and magazines. Walking along the shelves, he made a most unusual find himself—a copy of Lord Byron's early satire, *English Bards and Scotch Reviewers*, now suppressed by its author and out of print. He showed it to Nicholas, who wanted to know if there was another copy.

Mr. Highley looked up from the ladies' bills. "Could be, sir. Mr. Dunlevvy wouldn't put it out, for he held it in dislike."

"Why was that?" Langley asked.

"Ah, sir, it roasts the Whigs most proper, especially Lord Holland, 'n Mr. Dunlevvy couldn't forgive it."

Nicholas laughed. "Just like Mr. Dunlevvy not to forgive an insult to a Whig, even though Lord Holland himself seems to have done—Byron was received at Holland House, I hear."

"Yes," Langley agreed. "But he told me himself that the insult to Lord Holland is the reason he has refused to have the book reprinted."

"I heard it was to please Lady Melbourne," Miss Blackwood interjected pertly. Since this skirted perilously close to a scandal Lady Trumbull considered too shocking to discuss, she announced in loud tones, "Please, let us not discuss the antics of that odious man. His mother-in-law, Lady Millebanke, is a close friend of mine, and I simply cannot bear to hear another word."

Miss Blackwood pouted prettily, but she was in sufficient awe of Lady Trumbull to drop the subject. However, a wink from Nicholas made her eyes sparkle, and she turned aside to hide a giggle.

Highley located another copy of *English Bards*, and a

very satisfied group of customers exited M. Dunlevvy, bookseller. Gwynneth could hear the happy chatter from her office, for Langley had left the door ajar when he returned to the front of the shop. When they were all gone, the silence seemed oppressive. She came to the door and sighed, rubbing the back of her neck.

"Here, now, why the sad sound?" Mr. Highley waved a sheaf of notes in one hand and hefted a fist full of coins in the other. "That lot just bought more in a few minutes than we usually sell in a week."

Gwynneth smiled broadly. "Well, if the gentry returns to our shop, perhaps I may put away my red ink."

"Indeed so, Miss Gwynneth."

"But now I must go and order some of the newest merchandise from London, to have on hand if . . . no, *when* they return." With light steps she ran to the back, an optimism buoying her up that she hadn't felt since Charles had proposed. She hastily suppressed that bittersweet memory and threw herself into her bookkeeping.

Before she could make very much progress, however, she was annoyed to find Mr. Highley clearing his throat at the door. "Begging your pardon, miss, but there's a gentleman here to see you."

Expecting that Langley had returned, Gwynneth felt both apprehension and elation as she directed Highley to show him into her office. But to her astonishment it was a very different sort of man who strolled in and bowed to her. Exquisitely dressed and dandified, the auburn-haired gentleman had the look of one who thinks himself irresistible to women.

"Miss Dunlevvy? Sir Miles Barlow at your service."

Chapter Five

Sir Miles Barlow had an impudent eye, assessing Gwynneth quickly and rakishly. "I had thought my business would be with your father, but I confess I am not at all sorry to find myself in the presence of a lovely female instead."

Since this amounted to pleasure at finding her father dead, Gwynneth wasn't any more pleased with this speech than she was with the man's bold look. Standing, she asked him coolly, "What may I do for you, sir?"

"It may be a case of what I can do for you, my dear, at least in the end." Sir Miles gave her an insinuating smile and seated himself without being asked. "I came to discuss with you your publication, the *Guilford Register*."

"Excuse me, may I join this discussion?" Startled, both Gwynneth and Sir Miles turned to see Lord Langley entering her office door briskly, Mr. Highley ineffectually following to explain that he had tried to announce the man.

"Now why am I not surprised to see you here?" Barlow languidly surveyed Lord Langley through his quizzing glass.

"Well, I for one am surprised to see you both here. Sir Miles, I expect you are not aware that the *Register* ceased publication with the death of my father, over six months ago."

"Now, did it?" The man's voice seemed more amused than amazed.

"Of course it did. Father owned it and wrote most of it. It never made a profit, indeed it lost money consistently, so that we had to subsidize the salary of the printers to keep it going."

"We. Ah! So you *were* involved in it." Sir Miles smiled unpleasantly. Langley lounged against the shut door, his eyes hooded.

"Only in a very nominal sense. That is to say, I kept the books for my father, and . . . "

"And helped write some of his libelous, seditious articles?"

"Libelous! Seditious! Indeed, not. Or are you one of those people who see all criticism as sedition?"

"Miss Dunlevvy, I think I should warn you that Sir Miles Barlow is not expressing a personal interest in your father's newspaper. He is conducting an official investigation for the government. Though I still fail to see how you can prosecute a dead man, Miles, be he never so guilty."

"Prosecute! Guilty! My father was guilty of nothing but a desire to see justice done."

"A desire to see our enemies triumph abroad . . . "

"Not in the least. A desire to see the French have a constitutional monarchy as we have, not the reimposition of the Bourbon despotism."

"And our government overthrown at home . . . "

"Never! Though he saw its flaws, he thought our form of government the best the world had to offer."

"Did he indeed! Commendable. Too bad you did not continue that line when you took over the publication." Barlow had stood suddenly and loomed over Gwynneth's desk, menace in his tone."

"I told you, sir. Publication ceased with my father's death." Gwynneth stood, too, chin up and fists clenched.

"Yes, so you did. Which means you are not only a traitress, but a lying traitress."

Gwynneth's gasp of outrage was overshadowed by Langley's deep voice challenging Barlow, "Softly, Miles. I assume you have some foundation for such an accusation. Stop playing with Miss Dunlevvy."

Barlow turned toward Langley. "I suspect you know a great deal more about this than you pretend, Mr. Publishing Peer." This sobriquet, applied in ridicule to Langley in London, took on a sinister tone in Barlow's mouth.

"I know nothing about it."

"Then why are you here?"

"As Miss Dunlevvy's friend and as a disinterested friend of the free press."

"Free to print scurrilous libel. Yes, you and your ilk would like that! But it was my understanding that you only arrived in Guilford yesterday, so how came you to be Miss Dunlevvy's friend?"

"I am the friend of anyone I feel may be a victim of a repressive element in our government. I saw you ride up just as my party was leaving town, and decided to look in, because I knew you had come to Guilford for some sort of witch-hunt. After all, Miss Dunlevvy is a young female alone in the world, without anyone to protect her . . . "

"And you are taking her under your protection?" Much could be implied in that word, and Barlow's arched brow encompassed its least respectable implications.

"He certainly is not. Not in any sense of the word. I am a respectable female, and I don't need protection against the government, for I've done nothing wrong."

"Then you deny publishing a libelous, seditious newspaper."

"I told you, it was neither libelous nor seditious, but in any case it ceased publication with my father's death."

"Then perhaps you can explain these to me." Sir Miles reached inside his coat and withdrew several sheets of newsprint, which he tossed contemptuously upon her desk.

Gwynneth picked them up. Immediately she recognized the masthead of her father's newspaper, the *Guilford Regis-*

ter. At first her cheeks reddened, and then paled as she read. Abruptly she dropped the sheets as if they were on fire. "Sir, I cannot read such things. How dare you . . . "

"Scurrilous. Shame on you for handing such a thing as this to a lady." Langley had taken up the sheets immediately, and now shook them furiously in Barlow's face.

"Such a fine sensibility, Miss Dunlevvy. And yet, you published them, and probably wrote them, too."

"I couldn't write such things. I can't even bring myself to read them. And my father never printed anything like that. In spite of the masthead, this is some sort of imposition, a forgery."

"I think not. Though if your father has been dead six months, it is true enough that he could not have published it."

For the first time Langley noticed the dates on the mastheads. "March, 1814. April, 1814. May, 1814. Why, these are recent."

"How well you do surprise, Stuart. I must recommend you to Drury Lane."

"I've had about enough of your insinuations, Barlow." Langley's free hand grabbed Sir Miles's snowy cravat and jerked him up onto his toes.

"Please, Lord Langley, do not! If Sir Miles thinks I or my father would publish such things, he does right to hold us in contempt, but neither of us did. There is some kind of skulduggery here. Someone is using my father's paper's name to hide his own dirty work."

Barlow shoved away Langley's hand and smoothed his clothes. "You could find yourself in Newgate for interfering with an officer of the court, Langley."

"You'd look a fool to try that, Barlow. But if you'd like to settle it privately . . . "

"Dueling is illegal, too. You really should study some law, Stuart, if you are going to go around breaking it all the time."

"I hate to interrupt, gentlemen, but it has been a long day. Sir Miles, I know nothing of these publications, but I wish you good luck in running down the perpetrator. Honest, fair criticism of our government is one thing. Vile personal attacks like these are quite another."

"Then you still maintain you have nothing to do with these, Miss Dunlevvy?"

"Definitely not."

"Do you still own the press?"

"Yes, but . . . "

"Where is it located?"

"In a warehouse two blocks from here. But it has been closed and locked since my father's death. The printers have gone to others jobs. This wasn't printed there."

"If that is the case, you won't mind showing me the press, letting me have a look around."

"Not at all."

"Are you quite sure, Miss Dunlevvy?" Langley turned his dark brown eyes on her, full of concern.

"*Et tu*, Lord Langley? What an opinion you have of me, to be sure."

"I never thought you wrote or countenanced these, but . . . "

"And you were right. I have nothing to hide."

"Then take us there now, Miss Dunlevvy. Let me inspect the premises."

"Certainly." Gwynneth marched briskly around her desk and out the door. "Mr. Highley, where are the keys to the *Register*?"

"Oh, very good," Barlow said softly. "Another Siddons."

"Your father kept them in the safe, miss."

Gwynneth returned to her office and opened the heavy freestanding safe. She had paid little attention to it since her father's death, beyond locating his will and ascertaining that there were many bills in it, but very little money. "Here they are," she announced after feeling around on the tray at the top of the interior. She took them out and walked past the two men who where watching her. "Coming, gentlemen?"

The sun was low in the summer sky as they left the bookstore. Still, it was bright enough to make them blink as the three emerged. "Take my arm, Miss Dunlevvy," Sir Miles offered, favoring her with a syrupy smile. "I'll escort you."

"I can escort myself, thank you." She marched ahead of them, unaware of the appreciation with which the two men observed her skirts twitch in rhythm with her determined steps. "A pretty piece, eh, Langley? Perhaps she'd be grateful for my intercession with the court, do you think?"

"Damn you, Barlow, she is a decent young woman, and innocent, too. You saw how shocked she was by that material."

"I've seen many a budding actress who never got near a stage, Langley. Of course, you would maintain her innocence, as a bulwark against your own complicity."

"You're going to be sorry if these accusations continue."

"If you two can stop brangling, we are here." Gwynneth stopped in front of a rather dilapidated building with grimy windows through which it was impossible to make out anything. She tried several keys before finding the correct one, resolutely ignoring Barlow's sardonic grin. At last the lock gave, and she pushed the heavy door open. The three entered the dark room silently.

Through light filtered by the grimy windows, the press could be seen, a small one, surrounded by racks of type. Everything was in perfect order. Barlow lit some candles and taking a branch surveyed the room carefully. "Very neat, your father's pressmen. Everything put away carefully."

"Yes, so it seems. They had just finished an edition, the last week in December it was, when my father fell ill."

"Very tidy indeed." Barlow's eyes darted everywhere,

taking in every detail in the room, which smelled of oiled metal, sawdust, and printer's ink. "Where is your morgue?"

Gwynneth looked at him in bewilderment. "Morgue. I don't . . ."

"He means your file of back issues, Miss Dunlevvy."

"Oh. In the office in back." She led them through a door at the back, into a small inner room along one wall of which was a ceiling-high wooden case full of newspapers in pigeon holes. "Is that what you mean?"

Barlow made no answer, but began pulling out issues, muttering dates as he went. At last he stopped. "Well, I should have known you wouldn't keep recent copies here."

"I expect every issue for the last year is there," Langley observed. "That is the usual procedure."

"You know I mean those printed since January."

"There were none printed since December. I told you, my father . . ."

Barlow laughed, low and appreciatively. "You really think you've managed to fool me, don't you, Miss Dunlevvy." He sauntered to the front of the building, where to her intense surprise he summoned a pair of uniformed soldiers who were standing a discreet distance from the doorway. "Stand guard. Do not let anyone enter or leave these premises."

"I don't understand."

"I'd venture to guess Lord Langley does."

"No, Miles, for once you've left me behind."

"Each press has its own peculiarities, Stuart. A little more pressure on one side than the other, perhaps. Also, type becomes worn in characteristic ways as it is used. An analysis and comparison of the issues in Miss Dunlevvy's morgue with those I have here, and other samples of this scurrilous, libelous publication, should soon establish whether they were printed on this press."

Gwynneth drew herself up proudly. "I am very glad to

hear that, Sir Miles. In that case I will soon be completely exonerated."

"If you are, Miss Dunlevvy, I shall be more pleased than almost anyone, other than yourself, of course, to learn it. I'll have those keys, please." Sir Miles held out his hand and, when Gwynneth moved to drop the keys in it, seized her hand abruptly and carried it to his lips for a lingering kiss. "Your servant, miss." He made an elaborate leg, and raised eyes gleaming with lascivious meaning to meet Gwynneth's indignant stare.

Gwynneth snatched her hand away and walked hastily back toward her bookshop, her mind in a turmoil. She was hardly aware of Langley striding at her side until he said, "I know you are not involved in this mess, my dear. I do hope Miss Allen is not, for all our sakes."

This stopped her in her tracks. "Miss Allen?" For the last hour she had completely forgotten the quest that had brought Lord Langley into her life, overshadowed as it was by the even more unwelcome presence of Sir Miles Barlow.

"No, no, of course she isn't."

"I'm not so sure."

"Surely you couldn't believe her capable of writing such vile things?"

"No, but I read enough of the pages he showed us to realize that the entire paper wasn't that vulgar. There was a very genteel description of Guilford on market day on the inside page, that was very much in Miss Allen's prose style."

Gwynneth turned huge, frightened eyes to his. "There was?"

Amber, Langley thought. Her eyes are amber in the sunlight. For a moment he forgot everything else, gazing into those huge alarmed eyes. He shook himself at last and responded. "Yes, there was. Did she write for the *Register* previously? When your father was alive?"

"No, never." Gwynneth's mind raced. How had that

essay come to be printed in that horrid paper? Her father would never permit her to write for the *Register*, careful though he was to avoid infuriating the censors. He had been aware of the danger of government persecution, and had been determined not to expose her to any danger by involving her in his journalistic enterprise.

Gwynneth jerked her attention back to the present, aware that Lord Langley had taken her hand and was stroking it in a soothing manner. "I am sorry to see you so distressed by this matter, Miss Dunlevvy. But much as I would like to assure you that you are in no danger, I think you should look about you for a good lawyer."

"Why . . . why do you say that?"

"Did you not notice, Miss Dunlevvy. The neatness of the pressroom?"

"What of it?"

"Even if it had been left that clean when your father's last issue was printed, by this time there would be cobwebs here and there, wouldn't there? And dust?"

Gwynneth sagged against the building. "What . . . what are you implying, Lord Langley?"

"I believe your press has been used very recently. And I am sure that Sir Miles Barlow thinks so, too."

Chapter Six

The wind whirled through the cracks and crevices and howled around the chimneys as Gwynneth locked the shop door behind Highley at the end of the day. An approaching summer storm had darkened the sky to a sullen gray. Above stairs, her faithful former nurse Hannah Salton would have a cosy fire burning in the parlor and their simple supper waiting.

She let her mind dwell on these homely details to keep it from skittering off to the alarming events of the day and the task that faced her once Hannah had turned in for the night. She must read the note Lord Langley had written her in the shop the day before, the note she had first thrown in the dustbin, and sworn not to read. Why did that seem so long ago?

She had already decided to reply to it, even before Sir Miles Barlow's menacing presence entered her life. But now, in addition to taking pity on Lord Langley's obvious unhappiness at receiving no reply, was added her gratitude that he had been with her when Sir Miles confronted her. Something about that man, aside from his ridiculous charges, frightened her. Gwynneth had been flirted with many times before, and had learned to parry unwanted attentions quite effectively. But there was an aura of menace in Sir Miles's obvious interest that sent chills of alarm up her spine.

When her meal was consumed and the table cleared,

Gwynneth bade her longtime friend and servant good night. With a little quiver of anticipation, she retrieved Lord Langley's note and broke the seal.

> Dear Miss Allen:
>   I know a very great deal about you—yr taste in literature and music your moral position on slavery on war on this war on heaven and earth . . . your opinion of Prinny and Princes and Princesses and Principalities.
>   I know your wit and wisdom and ambition and also yr folly—at least one example of it which is refusing to let me know you as a living person and not a series of hieroglyphics on a page.

Gwynneth's progress in reading this missive was slow, because in addition to his usual disregard for punctuation, Langley's handwriting, under the pressure of the strong emotion he had been feeling, was even more chaotic than usual. She frowned and smoothed her brow with her forefinger as she read:

> You fear—what? Surely you know much about me through our correspondence is it not enough to assure you that if old I will revere you if young I will adore you if married I will respect yr vows—if you wish it—if single I will . . . but as to that I make no promises except that, whatever yr condition I will be yr friend.
>   I am in Guilford visiting Mr. Verleigh for a fortnight or so will you not reveal yrself to me—discreetly if you wish—the merest hint—can you really have me so close at hand and not know me?
>   Address yr response to Dunlevvy's bookstore and—dear Enigma—believe me ever yr wondering
>
>   L

Gwynneth tossed the note on the desk. He was a fine one to speak of hieroglyphics! Yet she had learned his hand so well—but not him. She frowned as she remembered that the note had been penned in her very shop, by the very rogue who, just moments later, had violently assaulted her and raised equally violently warring responses of anger and desire in her. If that event had never happened, she might well have given in to his persuasion and her own inclination, and made herself known to him. For that reason alone, she had to be thankful that he had shown her his true colors beforehand.

Yet, what were his true colors? He thought her no more than the impertinent bookseller through whom he would reach "Miss Allen," yet he had stood by her today even in the face of Sir Miles Barlow's thinly veiled threats that suspicion might fall on him if he aided her. It seemed to her to be the act of a brave, perhaps even a principled man, to stand up to Barlow, who had the authority of the crown and troops at his command.

With a sigh she moved to the inkwell. She meticulously prepared a pen and laid out paper, then sat staring into the dying fire. What to say? Though she had been careful what she revealed to Langley, she had tried not to lie to him. She didn't want to begin now. She must find some way to discourage his determination to know her identity. Probably the best way would be to hold out the promise of continuing the correspondence—this intellectual companionship that she cherished so much obviously was valuable to him, too.

At last she took up her pen and began, taking pains her copperplate was as neat and clear as she could make it.

Dear Lord Langley:

How I wish you would give up pursuing the chimera of acquaintance with me. It cannot be, and I cannot tell you why. To do so would reveal too much. You would guess the rest and, judging from your impetuosity as expressed on paper and to Miss Dunlevvy, expose me. I can only say that deeply though I value our correspondence, I cannot change it for an acquaintanceship which would disappoint you and endanger me.

To avoid complications, I shall not receive or write any more letters until you have left Guilford. When you return to London we may, if you wish, resume our correspondence upon the old terms.

I remain, sir, what I have always been, your humble and obedient *literary* friend.

Miss Suzanne Allen

Gwynneth reread the letter and sealed it with another sigh. Why did part of her hope it would fail of its purpose?

A turn or two around the room, and she was back at her desk. There was still time to write some of Lady Ridgeway's invitations for her, for the dinner and ball she was giving in honor of Mr. Verleigh's distinguished guests. Her ladyship had been particularly in alt to learn that Lord Langley was among the visitors to their county. Probably hopes he'll offer for her daughter, Gwynneth thought. Little does she understand the kind of man she is dealing with.

Some time ago Lady Ridgeway had seen Gwynneth's neat, elegant writing on a statement she had prepared for her father. The baroness had begun asking her to act as an amanuensis on occasion, as Lady Ridgeway herself had a shaky, unattractive, and difficult-to-read hand. She was, moreover, given to rather grotesque spellings.

The trifles Gwynneth earned in this way she husbanded as carefully as all her other resources, against the day she could go to London. If she couldn't support herself with her literary efforts, she might even, with Lady Ridgeway's recommendation, do copy work to enable herself to live independently in the great city.

Gwynneth was not without resources. Her grandfather, the Earl of Fenswicke, had left her a small legacy, and her mother's tiny dowry had come to her on her father's death. She had enough to live modestly well in a country setting, but Gwynneth was tired of country living. If she could sell the building and the inventory of the bookshop, she could invest the money in the funds and add another significant amount to her yearly income. What she could earn by her own efforts would give her added security. Thus she could afford to move to London, to what she hoped would be a more stimulating, congenial atmosphere.

She did not hope to recover all that her father had paid for the bookstore and print shop, because times had become harder and harder as the war dragged on, for all but the very wealthiest, so books and buildings alike sold poorly. Also, his radical views had driven off custom among the aristocracy, to the point that interested buyers would almost certainly lose interest after looking at the business's income.

So Gwynneth's first goal was to build up the shop's custom, that it might bring a decent price. Today's visit by Nicholas Verleigh's lively houseguests was a good step in the right direction.

Of course, if Sir Miles Barlow arrested her for libel and sedition, all of this hopeful planning would be for naught. But the charges are so ridiculous! Gwynneth's mind raced back and forth over her problems as she dealt with the rote task of copying the invitations.

Surely Sir Miles will quickly realize the whole thing is a mistake. Gwynneth managed to talk herself out of accepting Langley's advice to seek legal counsel. Lawyers are so expensive!

Having decided to await events, Gwynneth completed Lady Regina Ridgeway's invitations and put them with some books that were to be delivered to the baroness on the morrow. On the top she put several sheets of paper closely covered with her own writing. A smile softened her strained features as she thought about these summaries she had written.

Lady Ridgeway, in her own peculiar way, was a benefactress of Gwynneth's. Herself almost illiterate, she liked to appear au courant with everything when she rubbed shoulders with the aristocracy. As a result, she made sure her library contained all the books currently popular with the *ton*. She asked Gwynneth to include with each new book a brief synopsis, "to help me decide which ones I will want to read first."

Gwynneth knew that these brief "reviews" that she gave Lady Ridgeway served her well when conversation turned to books and authors, for it was doubtful that the baroness actually read even the tiniest fraction of the books she purchased.

Lady Ridgeway's bit of flummery had been very helpful. It produced a welcome windfall for her father's faltering business, gave Gwynneth some interesting mental exercise, and allowed her to read many books she otherwise could never have afforded to open. This in some measure compensated her for the loss of her grandfather's library, where she had run tame, even after his death, until her father's fatal sermon against reinstating the Bourbon king had alienated the family and cast them out into the world.

Lord Langley entered the bookshop the next day within an hour after Gwynneth had sent a local youngster with her message that a letter from Miss Allen had arrived for him. He took the missive from Gwynneth's hands so eagerly that she almost regretted depressing his hopes so thoroughly.

He strode to the window and read it, his eager look replaced by a scowl as he quickly scanned its contents. Crushing the paper into a ball, he returned angrily to her, ignoring the curious Highley.

"Do you have any idea what this says?" he demanded.

"No, my lord, I don't." Gwynneth cringed at the necessity for the lie, and something in her countenance may have belied her words, for his expression darkened and it seemed for a moment he might attack her. But he only bit out, "Indeed!" and stomped from the shop, throwing the offending letter to the floor.

Highley recovered the crushed paper and started to smooth it out. Gwynneth lept forward. "I'll take that, Ezekial. Perhaps Lord Langley will want it later."

"As you wish, miss." Highley nodded. His eyes were alive with questions, but Gwynneth didn't dare supply any answers. She turned to go to her office in back of the shop, leaving him to await customers.

Langley rode away from Guilford bitterly disappointed once again, but more determined than ever to smoke out this elusive poetess. He was not a man who liked to be thwarted. To his own intense desire to meet Miss Allen was added the possibility that she might be in danger. He was sure he recognized her style in the little essay he had read inside one of Sir Miles's newspapers. Whether she was knowingly cooperating with the publishers of that scurrilous rag or was, as he suspected, somehow unaware that they were using her writing, she must be warned and convinced of her danger. He must offer her his assistance, too.

He believed titles to be anachronistic, but as a peer of the realm he had certain resources that ordinary Englishmen did not. In addition, he had a modest amount of fame, and was not regarded with animosity by the Prince Regent, who thus far had taken his criticisms in good part, because Langley had taken care to balance them with praise where praise was due.

Their Prinny had exquisite tastes in art and very interesting ideas in architecture, and was personally charming and interesting. Langley felt perfectly justified in leavening his strictures on the government with praise of these qualities, both in print and in person, and the rather beleaguered prince had noted them. So an offer of assistance to Miss Allen if she were to be accused of a crime would not be an idle boast. He must find her, warn her, and convince her of his sincerity.

Surely such a well-educated woman as Miss Allen showed herself to be in her correspondence could not fail to attract notice in this small town. He would need to reveal some of his dilemma to Nicholas. No one loved solving puzzles more than his host. Perhaps his knowledge of the locals would help unmask her.

Nicholas was out with several other members of the party, shooting, when Langley returned. It was nearly dinner by the time Stuart finally ran him to ground and asked him for a private word in the library. There he briefly summarized his relationship with an unknown but very talented countrywoman, and put the question to Verleigh. "Do you have any idea who my mystery lady could be?"

Nicholas loved mysteries. Nothing pleased him better than to ferret out the unknown. He began firing questions at Langley, drawing out things he wasn't even aware that he knew about Miss Allen, until he had exhausted his small store of objective information.

"Really, I know more about her . . . spirit, I suppose is the right word, or soul. She has said little about herself or her situation in life, but her essays are delightful, and her poetry is, she once said, 'the breath of her soul.' At her best, she surpasses Wordsworth in her appreciation of your picturesque Lake Country, and Coleridge in her command of imagery. Occasional flashes of wit would compare well with Pope."

Astonished, Nicholas gasped, "You put her in high company, my friend."

"Indeed I do. She is modest about her gifts, but even I, who as you know do not shy away from intelligent women, am frequently amazed by her. And she is well-grounded in the classics, perhaps in their original language, and widely read in current literature."

"Someone with access to a substantial library, then."

"Yes, and an excellent classical tutor. I am convinced no typical lady's governess taught her."

"And you are sure she lives nearby?"

"Quite nearby. Miss Dunlevvy apologized for not having a reply for me by the next morning."

Nicholas paced a few moments, thoughtful. "We have few bluestockings here. Many young ladies write poetry, of course, as do their lovelorn swain. But you would toss their effusions to the wind as mere chaff, I am sure. As for a woman, especially a young woman, with the education you describe?" He shook his head in perplexity.

"I believe she is young, but perhaps I want to see her that way—young and beautiful."

"It almost sounds as if you are in love with her."

"You know me, Nick. I fall in love and out again with alarming frequency. I am more than willing to do so with this woman, if she be of an age and appearance to permit it. But there's more to it than that. With this woman I could be friends. 'Tis a state I treasure far above love, which never lasts and leaves only exhaustion and a rather nasty taste in the mouth after."

Nicholas laughed, shaking his head. "I'm not at all sure that what you are describing is love."

"Now, don't turn idealist on me, Nick!"

His friend's full rosy mouth turned up in a sudden quirk, and mischief lit his features.

"What is it?"

"A thought just occurred to me. What if this superbly educated woman isn't?"

"Come again?"

"Perhaps someone is making a May game of you. Perhaps it is a man."

With an oath, Langley quit his chair to stride across the room and stare out the window. "A clever hoax it would be, wouldn't it. Some of my enemies would dearly love to carry that off. And if they have, my letters must already be giving them infinite amusement."

He stood with bowed head, intent upon some inward vision. "But, no! You wouldn't suppose her to be anything but feminine after reading her letters and poetry."

Nicholas sighed. "That's what I need to do, right now, if I am to help you."

"The letters I don't have with me, but you already have several of her poems and essays, that is if you have subscribed to *The Legacy*."

"As if I dared not to!" Nicholas grinned up at his tall friend. "Even if I didn't read them out of interest, or for your sake, my sister would pester me until I knew no peace, did I not!"

"Sabrina and I have ever seen alike on women's abilities." Langley lifted his eyes to the portrait of Nicholas's vivacious older sister, married now and living nearby but a frequent visitor of her old home. "Shall I see her soon?"

"We will call on her, of course. Don't believe I've mentioned, she's breeding again. He husband keeps her very close, quite unnecessarily so, in her eyes."

Langley frowned and shook his head. "Why she must marry that stuffy Westcott, I cannot fathom. How she disillusioned me when she announced her engagement. I thought she was a true Wollstonecraftian woman."

"Thank God she doesn't take her ideals so far as you. I'm not quite ready for a sister with a bevy of bastards, and whether you like him or not, she was so besotted with Westcott that I'm sure that is what she would have presented him with if she hadn't married him."

A sudden thought illuminated Nicholas's face. "I say, perhaps it is Sabrina who is your mystery poetess? She certainly has the education, though she had to get it secondhand and by such subterfuges as doing my schoolwork for me."

"But why would Sabrina feel the need to hide her authorship from me? Would Westcott mind?"

Nicholas shook his head. "Doubt it. He's never objected to any of her other notions, as long as they don't endanger her health. Let her publish that book of wildflower drawings, didn't he? In fact, seemed proud of the recognition she received, too."

"It is a very careful botanical study of the flora of the Windemere region, Nicholas, not a 'book of wildflower drawings.'" Langley's irritation flared up. Even Nicholas wasn't perceptive enough to give his sister's accomplishment its just due. "But that's another reason to doubt her authorship of those poems. She is a natural historian and an artist, but I collect she never expressed herself well in writing."

Nicholas had to admit the justice of this observation. "I got quite a hiding once when I gave my tutor one of her compositions as my own. He said it was so inferior that I must have been disrespectful in my intentions in giving it to him."

"Still, Sabrina would likely know all the bluestockings in the area. She may know who my poetess could be. We'll ask her when we call on her. And let it be soon, Nick. There is a certain urgency to the matter." At his friend's interrogative look, Langley filled him in on Barlow's call on Miss Dunlevvy and the possibility that Miss Allen might be writing for the underground version of the *Register*.

"If it is as scurrilous as you suggest . . . "

"A most detailed and disgusting account of Prinny supposedly raping a virgin in his underground passageway at Brighton, among other things. I thought Miss Dunlevvy would faint when she began to read it."

Nicholas let out a long, low whistle. "Then your Miss Allen may not be the gently bred female that you suppose."

"What I suppose is that she was not aware what would be the other content of the newspaper when she became involved. By the way, have you seen any copies of the *Guilford Register* around here?"

"Not in its new incarnation. I was a subscriber, of course, to Mr. Dunlevvy's publication. But the first I heard of this one was when Sir Miles told us of it."

"I wonder where it is circulating, then?"

At that moment the dinner bell rang, and Nicholas swore softly. "Just this moment I wish my esteemed guests at perdition."

Langley laughed and clapped his friend on the back. "Poor old Nick, hates loose ends. Come, let us join the others. I shall point out Miss Allen's writings to you tomorrow morning, and you'll give me your opinion."

The next day found Nicholas and Stuart ensconced in the library at an earlier time that either was accustomed to rising.

Langley had a lively respect for his friend's intellect. He frequently called on him for literary criticism for his various publications, and the results were invariably insightful. Nicholas muttered to himself a little as he read. "Yes, I remember reading this one. I remember thinking she had caught the feel of Treswick Brook well, where it plunges so suddenly over the rocks and then drops into that quiet tarn."

He went carefully through all the poems and essays that had been published thus far, agreeing with Stuart as to their quality, but no nearer knowing their author.

"One thing, though. I am as convinced as you are that it is a female, if for no other reason because so accomplished a writer, if male, would long ago have won a name for himself. The style is unique. No one I know of who is currently writing would be able to do it as a hoax and resist using it in his known works. Too superior by far for a hack, too. And then, a three-year-long prank is beyond what one would expect of either friend or foe. Surely they would have sprung the trap by now."

All of this only confirmed Stuart's own opinions. He sat quietly listening as his friend ruminated.

"So, the letters are from a female, and genuine. Someone familiar with this countryside, too. And I agree with you that she is young—or was when she wrote them. There is a freshness to the experience, a naïveté to the language . . . "

"Yes, like someone noticing for the first time. You can't write that way at thirty. Too many experiences get in the way." A sudden thought illuminated Langley's grave features with joy. "Wait a minute! Perhaps it is Miss Dunlevvy!"

"That milk-and-water miss?"

"Yes. She is the right age, and surely literate." Langley rose from his chair, enthusiasm suffusing his features. "What do you think, Nick?"

His round face contorted in concentration, Nicholas slowly began shaking his head. "I don't think so."

"Why not?" Langley dragged a frustrated hand through his hair. How delightful it would be if the appealing young bookseller were his cherished correspondent. "I know you hate to think of me finding a solution before you do, but . . . "

"Several reasons occur to me but the most telling one concerns her father. Martin Dunlevvy was forever recruiting people to write for his paper. I made several contributions; so did almost everyone else around here who could read and write. He used to say a newspaper was a hungry beast, requiring words to keep it alive, and devouring them at a monstrous rate."

"Yet Miss Allen was never a contributor?"

"Not that I can recall. And as you say, her style is quite distinctive."

"As one who has to feed several word-devouring monsters myself, I can see where you are going with this. The man would scarcely have omitted printing every word of so talented a daughter's writing." Langley's shoulders slumped in disappointment.

"Unless she wrote without his knowledge."

"No, you are forgetting that charming poem in which she thanks her father for encouraging her to court her muse."

Nicholas wrinkled his nose. "Alas, I was. You seem to know her work almost by heart."

"But still, I'm no nearer knowing who . . . "

A scratch on the door and Nicholas's butler entered bearing the morning's mail on a tray.

"Thank you, Forbes."

Nicholas absentmindedly sorted through the stack as the taller man stood beside him, waiting impatiently until they could return to their task.

Suddenly Langley jumped. "What . . . let me see that envelope."

Nicholas shuffled back through the letters. "Which?"

"This one." Langley drew a large, expensive-looking letter with a crest on it from his host's hands. "This writing. It is hers! Miss Allen's! I'd know it anywhere."

Chapter Seven

Nicholas Verleigh stared at his friend as if he had taken leave of his senses. "This—the hand of the immortal Miss Allen? That I doubt. I know this crest." He took the letter back and broke the seal. "Yes, it's from Lady Ridgeway, a neighbor, wife of Arthur Metcalf, Lord Ridgeway." He scanned the page quickly. "An invitation to myself and my houseguests. She's giving a ball."

Langley clapped his hands. "That's it, then! This is her way of making an opportunity for us to meet."

"But *she* can't be your mystery woman, surely."

"Tell me about her." Langley's enthusiasm alarmed his friend.

"Gently, old man. Regina Ridgeway is a matron of around forty, a bruising horsewoman and pleasant hostess, but by no means the poetical type."

Not in the least deflected, Langley persisted, "Is she well educated?"

Nicholas hesitated. "Hmmm. She seems well-read, as regards current works, at least. Now I think on it, she often has a pithy, insightful comment to make about the latest book. But . . . I just can't see her writing poetry. Even when she was young. It's so far from her type, you see. An outdoorsy, horsey type, robust and not in the least introspective."

"But I swear this is her handwriting. She always makes of each letter a little work of art, almost like the old illuminated manuscripts. These little curlicues on the ends of each word are unmistakable signatures."

"Perhaps one of Lady Regina's daughters helped write the invitations. She has two, a chit of thirteen I know little about, and Virginia. She is seventeen and will make her come-out this fall."

"Are either of them intelligent? Who teaches them?"

"I hardly know. Of the younger one, I am in complete ignorance, as she isn't out, even in provincial society. The older girl is very pretty, and a fine horsewoman, like her mother, but I shouldn't have imagined her to be poetical. And I don't think their governess is anything out of the ordinary. I would look for the girls' education to be quite typical for our class."

"In other words, abominable. It couldn't be the younger one, at any rate. She would have been only ten when she first wrote me. And however young my correspondent may be, she is definitely a young woman and not a child."

"Then perhaps it is Virginia. Who can tell with a miss just out of the schoolroom? There could be depths unplumbed, hidden behind the awkwardness and the blushes." But Nicholas seemed unconvinced.

"I must meet them. This ball, is it soon?"

Nicholas studied the invitation. "A week and a little more. But we can call on them today, if you like, with our acceptance."

That very afternoon the two friends were shown into Lady Regina Ridgeway's drawing room. Langley studied both Lady Regina and her daughter Virginia carefully as he was introduced, but saw only a well-bred, polite matron and a pretty, slightly flustered young girl who seemed outwardly to be nothing out of the ordinary. If either of them was his secret correspondent, she was a clever dissembler.

Deciding the girl was too young and transparent for such art, he turned his attention to the mother. Attractive, though handsome rather than pretty, and impeccably groomed, she was poised, sure of herself, and socially adept. Surely here was his quarry. At last he was face-to-face with his "Miss Allen."

He tested the waters lightly. "I have been looking forward to making your acquaintance for some time, Lady Ridgeway."

There was a beat too long in her response, a look of surprise on her face, and then she answered, "And I you, my lord. No woman can fail to be grateful to the man who has given my sex a voice all our own in the literary world." She remembered Miss Dunlevvy's phrasing exactly, when she had praised Langley's new journal, *The Legacy*. She had been urging Lady Ridgeway to subscribe. It had been Gwynneth's comment that it was sure to be all the talk among the *ton* that had convinced the baroness to add it to her library.

Langley felt as if a thunderbolt had struck him. Miss Allen had said almost the exact thing to him nearly two years ago, in one of her early letters. Here at last was his long-sought-after correspondent, the prim yet wise and learned woman of the letters, the consummate wordsmith of the essays and poems, in the most unexpected of vessels, a fortyish matron with a hearty country manner.

He tried not to feel let down. For had she not warned him again and again that he would be disappointed and uninterested in her if they ever met?

And Langley *was* disappointed. In spite of his assurances to Miss Allen, to Nicholas, and to himself, he was more than halfway in love with his correspondent. His romantic vision of her had always been of some lovely, young, unattached female who would be free to return his love. He had supposed his vocal opposition to the institution of marriage had accounted for Miss Allen's unwillingness to make herself known to him. But here she was, married, older than he, and with nothing of the lover in her manner. Nor was there anything about her person to inspire the lover in him.

Lady Ridgeway was a little unnerved by the intense look on Lord Langley's face, but continued on, seeking to draw her daughter into the conversation and to the notice of this eligible young lord. "And my Virginia is an avid reader of your poetry, are you not, my love?"

Nicholas looked as surprised as Stuart felt. Much of the wicked Lord Langley's poetry was considered improper reading for such a young girl, and few careful mamas would admit to permitting their daughters such dangerous literature.

Virginia, flustered but well prepared, responded, "Indeed, Lord Langley. I have read 'Gravemont in New England' above a dozen times, I am sure. I am quite in love with him."

Since Gravemont was universally believed to be a thinly disguised version of himself, even as Byron was seen in his Childe Harold, Langley could only grimace at this disingenuous admission. A glance at Lady Ridgeway showed she did not disapprove of the speech.

Langley felt a sudden surge of disappointment. Was his soul mate to turn out to be merely a self-serving, matchmaking mama?

Nicholas knew his friend's temperament well, and quickly drew the Ridgeways into another line of conversation before ending the brief visit with a general acceptance of the invitation to Lady Ridgeway's ball. "All of my guests were charmed at the notion, and think it very condescending of you to give a dinner and a ball on such short notice."

Lady Ridgeway laughed. "I am exceedingly glad to have your party visiting nearby, since almost the whole of our local society has gone to London now." She turned to Langley. "I fear, sir, you may find it a paltry ball. Only about a dozen couples in all."

"I am not at all surprised, though, that you are not in London yourself," he responded, studying her face carefully for any reaction to his oblique reference to "Miss Allen's" disapproval of the plan to restore "Louis the Slug" to the throne of France.

"Oh, goodness, no, Lord Ridgeway would never go to London in the summer, though how you guessed it I am sure I don't know." Her look was more one of puzzlement than consciousness. "Indeed, he hates London at anytime; I quite wonder if I shall manage to drag him there for Virginia's come-out."

As they rode home, Langley was deep in thought and Nicholas left him to it until they neared his own estate. At last he could stand the suspense no more. "Well? What do you think?"

"Oh, it is her, without doubt." Langley smiled wistfully.

"Why do you think so?"

"That business about my giving her sex a voice in the literary world—it was almost a direct quote from one of her earliest letters. I wonder if it was inadvertent, or her way of revealing herself to me?"

"Not what you'd hoped for."

"Hang it all, no The fact that she is married doesn't surprise me. It would explain her unwillingness to name herself to me. But to immediately steer me to the daughter. It's so crass. And unwise, knowing how I feel about marriage, as she certainly does."

"Perhaps, in spite of appearances, the daughter hadn't been prompted?"

"Even if by some rare chance that is the case, I am satisfied Lady Ridgeway was not in the least discomfited by her daughter's remark. Seemed pleased, in fact."

"Ummm. Yes, I thought so, too."

"Odd. I had thought myself shockproof. But that particular poem was certainly not intended to be read by young ladies just out of the schoolroom. I would have thought she'd have better judgment."

The two rode on in silence. Then Langley brightened as they reached the steps of Verleigh Hall. "Perhaps it was a way of putting me off. After my frequent flirtatious remarks in the letters, doubtless she fears I'll make advances toward her. What's her husband like?"

"Everything you loathe, I expect. He certainly would not be a complacent husband, were his wife to take a lover, so her cautiousness can readily be understood. An alarmingly typical country squire, a real beefeater. John Bull personified."

"No! The thought of that marvelous spirit trapped in wedlock to such . . . " Langley threw himself from his horse and walked swiftly toward the house. "I need to be alone. I have much to think of."

Nicholas watched him go, worry making him nibble at his full lower lip. His friend was capable of acting very impetuously at times. Lady Ridgeway, he thought, had done well to hide her identity from him for so long. A premonition of unpleasantness to come caused a delicate shudder to run down his back.

Lord Langley entered the bookstore full of determination. He had spent the night going over and over in his mind the conversation with Lady Ridgeway and thinking about the letters she had written him. He was perplexed by the incongruity between the person he had met and the person he had come to know from her letters.

Especially puzzling was why she would so determinedly refuse to meet him, and then virtually identify herself to him in their first conversation, by quoting from one of her own letters. Was she deliberately making a May Game of him? Or subtly, perhaps unconsciously, asking for his help? He couldn't wait a week to see her; now she *must* agree to a private interview, for he knew her secret; hadn't she fairly shouted her identity to him?

Also, there was the matter of Sir Miles Barlow. She had to be warned of her danger, if she had written that essay, and assured that she had a powerful friend in him if it was traced back to her.

He had composed a letter which he knew was rather villainous, at least in its impact, if not in its intention. But he was determined to have his way in this, and if a little blackmail would accomplish that, so be it.

Mr. Highley greeted him and informed him that Miss Dunlevvy was not there. "She has gone for a walk, m'lord. Such a fine day as it is, I told her she'd been shut up in this shop too long. A fine lady like herself slaving over the accounts and ordering books. It's wrong, that's what it is. The old earl must be turning over in his grave."

Langley was less interested in Miss Dunlevvy and her progenitor than in getting his letter delivered, but this man might know something about the correspondence, and seemed in a talkative mood.

"The old earl," he prompted. "What earl would that be, and what has an earl to do with Miss Dunlevvy?"

"The Earl of Fenswicke. He was her grandfather." Mr. Highley's tone of voice was proud. "Right fond of her, he was, such a merry little thing and so clever. Her father was his youngest son and had a fine living as the vicar at Aynsdowne until His Grace died. She was ever in the library. I was the earl's librarian at the time."

"How came she to be a bookseller, then, with the Earl of Fenswicke as a doting grandfather?"

"The young earl that now is, his grandson, lived with his mother there at Aynsdowne after his father was killed in a carriage accident. She heartily disliked Mr. Dunlevvy. He was a Jacobin, she said, and a bad influence on the parishioners of the church, not to mention her son. The sentiment was shared by Lord Walde, her second husband, a vain old fool who loved to prate of battle and boasted some kinship with the Bourbons. After the old earl died, Mr. Dunlevvy preached a fine but ill-judged sermon against the policy of restoring the Bourbons to the throne . . . "

"Good man," Langley muttered.

"Yes, and so say I, but they were the guardians of the young earl, and as such held the living in their hands. They threw him out."

"Villainous."

"As you say, sir. A pair of vipers. I came here with Mr. Dunlevvy, when he determined to leave the cloth and enter trade. He thought to help influence minds by selling books and publishing pamphlets against the war and the restoration. Wrote some of them himself. Almost got arrested for sedition. There was always some government spies about."

"Yes, I have heard of the *Guilford Register*."

Mr. Highley looked surprised. "Didn't know its fame had spread to London. Thought that was the only reason he wasn't closed down, because it was so obscure."

"The subject came up at Mr. Verleigh's the other evening."

"Ah, I see. Mr. Verleigh was always most supportive of Mr. Dunlevvy, no matter how radical Mr. Dunlevvy became. 'Twas a good little paper, too."

Highley chuckled fondly at his memories. "He was happy as a clam, leading the government censors a merry chase. Always careful never to cross the line, you see, but skated devilish close. Never really cut out to be a clergyman! Too much of a free thinker and bon vivant."

Highley paused here to mop his brow with a large white handkerchief. "Yes, we hoisted many a cup together. But for Miss Dunlevvy, I fear, it was an evil day."

Langley was somewhat confused. "The day he published the *Register*?"

"Oh, no, sir. The day he left the clergy and went into trade."

"It must have been hard on her, to lose her home and her place in society."

"Indeed it was, sir. And that wasn't all she lost. No, sir, that wasn't the worst of it." Highley shook his head morosely.

Here the clerk had to pause to sell a book on diseases in cattle to an earnest-looking young farmer.

Langley found himself diverted by the tale. Miss Dunlevvy's reserve and fierce pride owed much to this fall from privilege, he guessed.

Highley returned to the tale eagerly when prompted. "Yes, sir, Mr. Dunlevvy's descent into trade cost her dearly. She'd been attached to Charles Osgood, son and heir to Viscount Dirksmansville, a fine young man whose land marched next to her grandfather's. They had an understanding, though she was too young for an engagement, her father thought."

"How old . . . ?"

"Just seventeen when it all came to a head. They'd begun courting when she was but fifteen. When we first moved here, young Charles rode over several times, and wrote to her frequently. It seemed he would stand by her. But his father made him give her up. He married another girl last year. Aye, that was a sore day for our Gwynneth."

"And not long after, her father died."

Highley nodded his agreement to this calculation.

"She has been battered about. Is she bitter against him?"

"Her father? No, not a bit of it. She was proud of him for his courage, though she didn't always agree with his ideas. A very independent mind, has Miss Gwynneth, and not afraid to speak it. And as for that traitor Osgood—she was better off without a husband with so little backbone. But she was very low, for a while, and no mistake."

Highley looked around the book-filled room. "I'll be glad when she sells this wretched shop. She should go to one of her cousins and live like the lady she is. Though so proud as she is, she may never do so. Certainly after the funeral, she refused all offers of assistance from those who had turned their backs on her father."

Langley was moved by this tale, and doubly sorry for his assault on the girl. How her pride must have been stung by his behavior. He marveled she'd been able to show him any courtesy at all since. He understood now her loyalty to Lady Ridgeway, who obviously had befriended a sadly friendless young woman. This returned his thoughts to his original purpose.

"Did you know she's been acting as a go-between for me, forwarding letters to and from a lady of my acquaintance?"

Highley's astonishment was obvious. Suddenly he remembered tales he'd heard of this dangerously handsome dark-haired lord. "The need for secrecy suggests a married lady?"

At Langley's nod of assent he burst out, "Not in her line, not at all. Can't imagine her lending countenance to anyone circumventing their marriage vows. 'Twas a point of argument with her father, who questioned the institution of marriage, being somewhat under the influence of Godwin, you see. And his own marriage had been none too happy, I collect, though his wife died many years ago."

"I would I had known the man. He sounds very much to my liking."

"Yes, well, Miss Dunlevvy, for all she loved her father, is a very straight-laced young lady. A strong Christian, too. She stoutly defended marriage to him and held forth against any who would weaken it. And you say she helped you in a clandestine correspondence? Amazing."

Langley frowned. "It really isn't as improper as it sounds. Our subject matter, you see, is primarily poetry. The lady in question writes in secret, for reasons I've yet to determine, and sends her poems and essays to me. I've published some of them in my literary magazine."

"Ah, well, that would explain it, I suppose. Allowing that Miss Gwynneth knows that is the purpose of the correspondence."

"I have reason to believe she does. Also, perhaps she continued to forward the correspondence after her father died because it was begun under Mr. Dunlevvy's aegis. You may have seen the letters, known to whom he gave them?"

He lifted his heavy eyebrows encouragingly. "I'd give a monkey to know who receives them." He made a gesture to his pocketbook. "They were addressed to a Miss Allen, in care of M. Dunlevvy, Bookseller."

"No." Highley was definite, though his eyes followed Langley's hand with avid interest. "'Twas always Miss Dunlevvy who dealt with the post. Her father would never allow her to work in the shop, but he let her help him with business in every other way. He had little interest in the accounts or ordering or other such details. She must have at least known about it all along."

"Still, she would have done as her father wished?"

"Oh, she was biddable enough. A dutiful daughter."

"For which I am grateful." Langley straightened away from the counter he had been leaning on as a customer entered the shop.

"Do you think she kept the *Register* going in obedience to some deathbed wish of his?"

Mr. Highley's astonishment was obvious. "Kept the *Register* . . . why, no, m'lord. The *Register* stopped when her father fell ill. Indeed, it fell to Miss Gwynneth's uncomfortable duty to let go the printers, as she could not afford to continue paying them. Couldn't even give them a severance, which led to some very hard feelings in these hard times, though no one felt worse about it than Miss Gwynneth."

"Hard feelings?"

"My, yes. One of the pressmen was a flame-haired Irishman who occasionally contributed an article to the paper. He wanted her to continue publication and wouldn't believe she couldn't afford to do so. He threatened her, he did. I had to throw him out bodily."

Langley tried not to show his amazement at this. The slender, slightly stooped Mr. Highley was almost fifty, surely. What hair he had left on his head was as gray as his long, thin mustache. But he knew that some men possessed a certain wiry strength not suggested by their outward appearance.

He had heard what he expected to hear regarding the *Register*. He was now completely convinced that Miss Dunlevvy was not involved in the recent scurrilous issues. Surely Sir Miles Barlow would realize that, too.

Unfortunately, the same could not be said with confidence of "Miss Allen." Now that he knew she was Lady Ridgeway, he was less sure that she was incapable of being involved with the scurrilous new incarnation of the *Register*.

"Where might I find Miss Dunlevvy? I wish her to pass on another letter for me. And naturally, this is something I would prefer you not speak of to anyone else."

"Naturally. In any event, wouldn't want to put Miss Gwynneth in a false light," Highley averred loyally. For a moment it seemed that the clerk would not tell Miss Dunlevvy's whereabouts, but the baron's penetrating, determined stare mastered him. "She and the vicar's daughter took a picnic and were going to walk along the banks of Windemere. Just ride along the western edge, and you can't miss her."

Chapter Eight

As Langley urged his bay gelding along the sedgy verge of Lake Windemere, he thought over the tale Highley had told of Miss Dunlevvy. A pity she had not acquired her father's Godwinian views about marriage. Had she read Wollstonecraft? An attractive young woman in her position might live a very interesting life if she could just throw off the chains of convention.

He wouldn't mind helping her enjoy her freedom himself, in fact. Langley smiled as he remembered her womanly curves, revealed to him as he had pressed against her that first meeting in her bookshop. Though she had emphatically rejected his advances, it hadn't been because she was repulsed by him, he was sure. His rough approach had frightened and angered her, and no wonder. But it was his experience that the spark of attraction rarely existed only on one side. If he hadn't been so involved with his mystery correspondent, he might already have made a push to make Gwynneth Dunlevvy his *chère amie*. He would enjoy seeing those unusual yellow eyes glow with passion.

But he had more important game in sight now. Far more important to him than a liaison based on mere physical attraction was the development of his friendship with the wise, witty Miss Suzanne Allen, now revealed as Regina, Lady Ridgeway. Miss Dunlevvy must deliver the letter in his vest pocket to Lady Ridgeway. Whatever the two women's means of communication, it appeared to be husband-proof, and he owed the lady that, at least for now.

By the calm banks of Windemere, Gwynneth and her friend Mary Humphrey were walking at a leisurely pace back toward Guilford, after a thoroughly satisfying day spent walking, reading, picnicking, and exploring the natural beauty of the lake area.

Mary was an intelligent girl who encouraged Gwynneth's plans to go to London and live a literary life. She was one of the very few who had been allowed to read some of Gwynneth's poetry, and was vastly impressed. She wavered between joining her talented friend or marrying a young clergyman who lived nearby. Their plans for the future occupied the two young women as they strolled home.

"But if I turn down Mr. Danvers and go with you to London, Gwynneth, you'll surely meet someone and marry, and I'll be left alone."

Gwynneth wrinkled her nose. "Who would marry me? I'm soiled by trade, have no fortune, and little claim to beauty. But if you love Mr. Danvers, you must marry him. I certainly would marry, if I loved someone who would love me in return."

Why did a memory of chocolate eyes and high-arched black eyebrows suddenly come into her mind? Gwynneth shook her head as if to toss the image of Lord Langley away, when suddenly it materialized in the form of a tall, commanding figure on a big bay gelding.

Dismounting, Stuart made a low, respectful bow. "Miss Dunlevvy."

"Lord Langley!" Gwynneth realized she was staring and adjusted her bonnet, which had fallen awry. "I'd like to present Miss Mary Humphrey, daughter of our vicar." She eyed him curiously, warily, as he saluted her friend with a kiss on the hand. Mary, flustered, curtsied low and wobbled a bit in the tall grass before retrieving herself.

"You've chosen a lovely day for an outing." Langley

gazed out over the placid waters, his eyes as troubled as the lake was calm. He fell into step beside Gwynneth, leading Turk.

They made small talk for half an hour as they walked, but finally Lord Langley could control his impatience no longer. "May I have a word with you privately, Miss Dunlevvy? A minute, no more," he promised Mary as she obligingly moved away.

Gwynneth watched her go uneasily. What business could Lord Langley have with her? Surely the meaning of her last "Miss Allen" letter to him had been unmistakable.

Her curiosity was soon satisfied as Langley brought out a sealed note. "You must deliver this to 'Miss Allen' for me right away." He gave a satiric emphasis to the name.

"I . . . I can't do that."

"Why not?" Stormy eyes fixed her, and she felt a tremor of apprehension.

"You know why."

"As do you, it seems. You are in her confidence, aren't you? 'I'll forward this to her' indeed. All you had to do was dash over there and hand it to her in person. And she told you not to do so while I was in the area, didn't she?"

He grabbed her arms and gave her a little shake. "Didn't she? She was afraid I'd follow you, or your messenger, that you'd lead me right to her."

Too astonished and perplexed to reply, Gwynneth stared at him openmouthed. Which discomposed her more, his large warm hands on her arms, or the things he was saying, she couldn't have told.

Abruptly loosing her, he turned to the lake and stared off into the distance. "It was very cleverly done. Her husband might see the post, but you can come and go as a friend, or deliver books perhaps."

Gwynneth drew in her breath at the words "her husband." What was he thinking?

Hearing the small gasp, Langley turned and gave her a

shrewd look. "Yes, I've guessed who she is. But I'm not willing to wait until the ball to talk to her. I've played her game, been her puppet, long enough. This note informs her where and when to meet me. If she does not, I'll expose our correspondence to her husband."

"No!" Gwynneth stepped forward in distress. Whoever he thought was Miss Allen, he could harm her greatly by telling her husband she'd been in secret correspondence with a notorious rake and freethinker.

"Yes, Miss Dunlevvy. And make sure your friend knows I mean what I say." Langley turned abruptly and began to mount his horse.

Gwynneth recovered her tongue. "Lord Langley, you are mistaken. You haven't found Miss Allen, and you are going to do someone a terrible harm."

"How do you know I haven't found Miss Allen when I haven't told you her name?" A sneer marred his handsome countenance. "Come, Miss Dunlevvy. You've played her game well, but it's over. One last message delivered by you, or I'll deliver the next one, in person."

"You selfish monster. Who would have guessed from your charming, beguiling letters what a selfish, self-centered brute you are!" Fury made Gwynneth bold—and careless.

"Ah, so she has shown you my letters, has she? That was poorly done of her. Those letters were confidential."

"And false, you . . . you beast. In them you are all that is considerate and respectful of females, whereas in reality you are a typical self-centered, domineering male!"

Langley frowned. "Not false. I am not an easy person to know, Miss Dunlevvy. But I flatter myself that my 'Miss Allen' has the intelligence and sensitivity, the openheartedness, to accept me with my many faults, when she knows me better."

"'Miss Allen' knows you well enough *now* to know she does not want to know you better."

The memory of their first meeting lay behind that vehement "now," Langley knew. He stiffened with anger. "Been carrying tales, haven't you? Well, carry this one: I will do as I threaten. Tell her to meet me, or else!" He lifted his reins, spurred his horse, and left Gwynneth standing, furious and frightened, as Mary hurried over, full of curiosity.

Her hands balled into fists, Gwynneth muttered, "My father warned me. He warned me again and again. I now know just how right he was."

"Whatever is going on, Gwynneth? You look pale as a ghost. What can you and Lord Langley have to shout at one another about?"

"Oh, Mary." She turned to her friend in dismay. "It is a long story, and I really can't explain right now, but I must get back home right away."

The letter seemed to burn in her hand. Some unknown woman was in danger because of her. If Langley told the husband that his wife had been writing him, who knew if the harm such an accusation caused could ever be undone, no matter how hard Gwynneth tried to explain.

She knew she must find out a way to deflect Langley, but exposure of herself as his correspondent was more frightening to her than ever. Clearly she was dealing with a ruthless man who would not respect propriety or the feelings of others if they interfered with his own wishes.

And what were his wishes, she wondered as she hurried home. He had always teased in the letters that he would make love to her if she wished, but he had also assured her that if she did not, friendship would delight him as well. "Friendship lasts longer," he had written. He had made it clear that he despised the institution of marriage and regarded lifetime monogamy as an unnatural state for both men and women. He had hinted darkly at cruel tyranny visited on his own mother by his violent father, and had cited case after case in which women were treated as chattel by husbands, undeterred by any English law.

Their spirited debate about the institution of marriage had never changed her mind, however, so he had always teased that if she would but grant him a personal interview he would convince her it was an outmoded, unnecessary barrier to a true relationship between men and women.

Since the morning he had assaulted her in the bookstore, she now had a better idea than ever of how he would go about "convincing" her. She doubted she was proof against his lovemaking. That was a frightening enough thought. But worse, she wasn't at all sure the man wouldn't use force if necessary to gain his way.

Hannah, distressed at her mistress's stormy face, begged her to confide what was wrong. "Nothing, I just seem to have the headache; perhaps too much sun." Gwynneth avoided her old friend's too-discerning eyes as she uttered this untruth. "I'll be all right and tight when I have rested a bit."

As soon as she gained the privacy of her bedroom, Gwynneth read Langley's letter, her heart beating madly with anxiety.

Dear "Miss Allen:"

At long last I have beheld your face and spoken with you—and yet I feel I know you even less than before I understand now yr concern about meeting me you are not old nor ugly as you once teased me but you are obviously very married and I will respect yr wish to continue that most permanent and confining of relations if you will respect my need to speak to my friend directly without the filter and barrier of written communication.

Moreover, a matter has recently come to my attention that places you in danger It concerns a certain essay of yours on market day in Guilford—I dare not say more in writing—but believe me when I say the danger is real and present—and I may be able to assist you.

I resent being treated like some wild beast liable to drag

you to my den and ravish you. I am determined to set our friendship on a new direct footing and if you will not meet me to discuss how best this may be done without alienating yr husband then I shall claim you for my longtime friend and correspondent quite openly for all to see at the ball on Friday.

I understand you ride daily—meet me just past the stone bridge where Lord Verleigh's north farm abuts the pinewood and we will ride together a space I will be there at 2 p.m. tomorrow.

Never yr obedient but always yr affectionate

L

This was dreadful. Gwynneth still did not know who Langley thought was Miss Allen, but whoever she was, Gwynneth knew she must prevent any harm coming to her, even if it meant revealing her own identity to the impetuous lord at last.

She felt so much trepidation at this course of action that she determined to make one more attempt to reason with Langley first. She would take a letter to this rendezvous, and if it did not convince him to leave the woman he supposed to be "Miss Allen" alone, she would then have to tell him the truth.

It would be difficult to reach the meeting place he had designated, even if she had a carriage at her disposal. Obviously his candidate for "Miss Allen" was a horsewoman, for the only way she could get to the rendezvous was on horseback—and she had no horse.

Stuart was restless and cross at Nicholas's that evening. He found it difficult to admit to himself, but his conscience was troubling him. Miss Dunlevvy's words still rang in his ears: "selfish, self-centered, and cruel." That last word stung particularly. Honest introspection revealed himself to be occasionally selfish and often self-centered, but certainly he wasn't cruel. Was he?

A spasm of grief gripped him at the memory of the cruel treatment by his father that had resulted in his beloved mother's unhappiness. He often morbidly watched his own behavior for dreaded signs that he was like his father, and found them more often than he liked. But surely to insist on furthering this once-in-a-lifetime friendship was not cruel?

Yet—perhaps to an outsider like Miss Dunlevvy, his actions seemed cruel. Lady Ridgeway, who had all of his letters, who had written him so many confiding, charming, trusting letters herself, wouldn't think so. Wouldn't she understand that he deserved her trust—that he would never purposely harm the writer of those letters?

And yet . . . how could she trust him when he had threatened public disclosure, which very well might destroy her marriage. Her marriage! That it might come first with her rankled with him, somehow. He wanted her to choose *him*, his friendship, over her marriage. He was jealous of her husband and her fidelity to him. How could he feel this way, when he didn't feel any attraction for Lady Ridgeway's person?

Oh, she was well-looking enough, growing a little stout, but still handsome. Their slight age difference wouldn't matter—he had had lovers older. But he did not feel the vibration, the physical spark he needed to feel to want her in that way. The spark, he realized in dismay, that was there very strongly when he was around Miss Dunlevvy. When he had grasped that young woman's arms to shake her this afternoon, he had very nearly forgotten his purpose and given in to the temptation to pull her to him and kiss her.

Perhaps he should have let Lady Ridgeway know that. Somehow he should have assured her that what he wanted from her was platonic friendship. And yet, how could he say to a woman, "You don't appeal to me." And what if, on better acquaintance, she *did* appeal to him? Then it would seem that he had lied to her.

Lost in his own reverie, Langley paid little attention to

Lady Morley during the evening. She had been attempting to set him up as her flirt, and had made it abundantly clear that he was welcome to come to her bed. He was surprisingly uninterested in doing so, being too intent on locating and running to earth his "Miss Allen."

After the evening's obligatory entertainments of piano playing, singing, and recitations, the party began to break up for the night. Lady Morley came to him as he arose from the chair where he had been sunk in reverie.

"Lord Langley, I would that I knew where you were this evening, for you were not with us."

He looked down into her lovely face, dominated by fine gray eyes under suspiciously dark lashes and high-arched brows. Her blond hair was arranged fetchingly with one long curl draped over her nearly bare shoulder. In the soft candlelight, she wore her nearly forty years lightly. She was a very desirable woman, and knew it. Still, no spark of desire impelled him to take up the invitation on those soft lips.

"Then the loss was surely mine." He bowed to her gallantly but moved away.

Lady Morley moved beside him again, pique at his indifference making her bold. "Your words are kind, but they make your actions even more cruel."

He turned, arrested by the word. "You are the second woman to call me cruel today, madam." For one, cruelty seemed to lie in too much attention, for the other, in indifference, he thought wryly. "But I assure you, I mean no unkindness. I am just a man with a great burden on my mind. I beg you will forgive me." He raised her hand to his lips in a parting salute and moved on.

When he reached the top of the stairs, a soft voice startled him at the very door to his room. "Perhaps you need someone to share your burden with?" He whirled around to find that Lady Morley had followed him. Langley was truly irritated. He liked to do his own chasing. This sort of predatory amorousness left him wishing a woman, no matter how lovely, in perdition.

"I seriously doubt you will want to assist me in convincing another woman that I love her," he sneered.

Lady Morley drew back, shock and anger written on her face. "I beg your pardon, Lord Langley. I have not become a procuress." With a haughty lift to her chin, she swept past him. He watched her go, wondering at his state of mind for passing up such a tempting morsel.

Chapter Nine

Under a lowering sky that threatened rain every minute, Stuart's horse chomped at short grasses on the forest's floor while his master stood impatiently at its verge, waiting for Lady Ridgeway. His frowning gaze was directed toward a small path that led through the woods.

When he had told Nicholas of his plan to force Lady Ridgeway to meet him, his friend had been quite worried. "You don't know the lady's husband, Stu. You could literally be endangering her life if he suspects an assignation."

"Then he mustn't suspect. Tell me how I can meet her without being observed."

After some deliberation, Nicholas had suggested this meeting place. She could enter the woods from her land, and ride unobserved to meet Langley within the woods, which he would enter from Nicholas's.

At last, considerably past the two p.m. deadline, Turk raised his head from his grazing to whinny a welcome to an approaching horse. Unexpectedly, the big bay faced outward toward the meadow, rather than toward the forest path as he trumpeted his greeting.

Whirling around, Stuart saw a rider approaching, but as the figure drew nearer he realized it could hardly be the one he was expecting. For one thing, the horse was a nag, slow-going and ungainly. Surely Lady Ridgeway would have a fine-blooded horse and sit it well, with her reputation. Then, the figure was slighter, and the hair lighter. "Damme if it ain't Miss Dunlevvy." Langley strode out of the trees and hailed her.

As Gwynneth turned toward Langley, her heart sped up with fear and a curious sort of exhilaration. He looked so handsome, so remote and unattainable, staring at her disapprovingly. Yet she, if she chose . . . in fact, if she wasn't very careful, she could have this magnificent man for her lover.

Her livery stable nag was more than agreeable about stopping. She had suffered considerable embarrassment and difficulty in hiring it, when she never had hired a horse before. "I wish to ride. I haven't done so in a long time," she had explained to the reluctant hostler.

"Ye know how?" He had been clearly skeptical.

"I am an excellent rider," Gwynneth had asserted.

Finally he had been persuaded to let her have the oldest, most decrepit nag in the stable, and a sidesaddle that seemed in imminent danger of disintegrating. He had grunted his disapproval when she refused to hire a groom to accompany her.

As she had not had occasion to ride in the last several years, her only riding habit was not in the black appropriate for her bereavement, but a deep forest green. it was a little tight across the bosom—her figure had matured since the day she had first worn it at sixteen. Charles had said it was very becoming, but Charles had said many things.

Gwynneth dismounted with Langley's assistance and led her horse into the cover of the woods. She did not wish to be observed meeting the wicked Lord Langley alone, if it could be helped. Langley followed her silently until she turned to face him.

The look on his face was enigmatic. His eyes ran over her features, her figure, missing no detail, she was sure. She felt stripped bare by that look, and quite defenseless. To end his scrutiny, she thrust a sealed letter at him.

He took it but continued looking at her, his eyes holding

hers in a mesmeric stare. "If she thinks to distract me with a surrogate," the deep voice began.

"No, not at all. Read the letter. I am to take a reply."

He frowned, then opened the seal and turned away to read. There was no salutation.

How shall I address you? You who were my friend, or so you said, and now announce your determination in the name of friendship to destroy my life. You have become my enemy. My dear enemy now, but if you carry out your threat, my hated, my despised enemy ever after.

Surely you cannot be so cruel as to deprive me of husband, family, position, pride. Yet I knew, I was warned, how dangerous you were, how careless of convention.

You are so impatient with the conventions that you say bind and enslave women that you sometimes act as if they don't matter. But they do—to me—because they matter completely to those around me, those to whom I owe both love and duty.

I approached you anonymously, to be careful. I hoped to fill a lack in my otherwise full and rewarding life—to find an outlet for my writing. Your letters lulled me with their friendly, beguiling tone. I responded to the offer of intellectual companionship, and opened my hidden heart to you.

Now you propose to take that heart out and trample it in public, or wear it on your sleeve like a trophy. Oh, cruel and selfish—can you be thus? I pray not. I pray you will meet me at the ball Friday as a stranger, and seek no more from me there, or while you are in Guilford, other than the merest nodding acquaintanceship, as you surely would not if I had never written you.

Then when you return to London, I can take up my pen again to address the only one to whom I have ever dared expose my poetic self.

Believe me, dear Lord Langley, that is all I can offer you. Take more and you destroy me.

I implore you to allow me to remain

"Miss Allen"

P.S. I have never written an essay on market day at Guil-

ford. Thus, whatever danger you believe such an innocu-
ous-sounding composition could create is nonexistent.

Lord Langley stood with his head bowed, ashamed of
himself, his thoughts uncomfortably self-accusatory. Noble
creature, frightened and fighting for her life, which *he* had
threatened with his heedless selfishness. Miss Dunlevvy
certainly had him there.

Recalling her, he turned to find Gwynneth watching him
anxiously.

"She is very eloquent, is she not?" Langley voiced the
pride he felt in his correspondent.

Afraid to speak, Gwynneth waited. He drew near her, the
large brown eyes darker even than usual, dark with emotion. At last he spoke. "Tell her I will do as she asks. You
are a good friend to her, Miss Dunlevvy. An unlikely pair-
ing, but then she is an unlikely authoress of these marvelous letters and poems."

"Yes. A woman must sometimes hide a great deal to fit
into a man's world." Gwynneth drew in a relieved breath.
The crisis had been averted!

Langley nodded and then shook his head like one coming out of a trance. His expression lightened, a teasing light
coming into his eyes. "And what are you hiding, Miss Dunlevvy? What lies behind those golden eyes that green becomes so well?" He moved closer, and Gwynneth stepped
back, one hand raised as if to ward him off.

She felt emotionally drained, relief at his agreement only
slowly replacing her fear. With great effort, she strove to
keep her tone light.

"I am hiding a strong desire to leave this compromising
situation behind. I'm not eager to be seen in an apparent
assignation in the woods."

"Ah, propriety again. *Et tu*, Miss Dunlevvy? Do you
have so much to lose by being seen with the wicked Lord
Langley?"

"It's nothing to do with you personally, my lord. The tabbies would tear me apart if I were seen in this situation with any man."

Langley continued to draw near. Gwynneth backed up until she made contact with the solid warm flank of his gelding. She jumped, and Turk started and turned his head, blowing indignantly at her before sidestepping and dropping his head to champ at the tender grass again.

Langley reached out and drew her toward him. "Take care. He's been known to kick. I wouldn't want you hurt."

"Then stand aside, my lord, and let me mount my horse."

"I was angry when I thought Lady Ridgeway had sent you for a surrogate. But you are a very fetching surrogate. That green habit reminds me why I detest mourning clothes."

Unnerved by his closeness, the warmth, solidity, and scent of male subduing her senses, Gwynneth stood mute, wide eyes fixed on him. He was going to kiss her, and somehow she must resist him. Her eyes strayed momentarily to his sensuous mouth, then hastily, nervously back to his compelling brown eyes, searching them for intentions.

After a long, tense moment his full lips quirked upward, and he dropped his hands. "Go, golden eyes. You have been a true friend to Lady Ridgeway and thus to me. I won't distress you further. Tell her to be completely easy in her mind. For once I shall be the soul of discretion."

Relief battled with disappointment as Gwynneth hastily caught up her horse's reins and with Langley's assistance mounted. Looking down at him, she smiled, a radiant smile from the heart. The crisis was averted! "You have chosen the right way. I am . . . Lady Ridgeway is going to be very grateful."

From the safety of her horse, she dared to prolong the meeting to satisfy her curiosity. "What made you . . . how did you know 'twas Lady Ridgeway? Was it anything I said or did?"

"No, be easy in your mind on that score. It was her handwriting."

Gwynneth wrinkled her nose in perplexity, a vision of Lady Ridgeway's scribble flashing before her mind's eye.

"The invitation to her ball arrived while I was conferring with my host. Her writing is unique and unmistakable, as I'm sure you will agree."

"Yes, it certainly is." Gwynneth put her hand to her mouth, stifling a slightly hysterical urge to giggle. "Was that all that convinced you?"

"That and a comment she made when we were introduced that was word for word what she had written to me in her first letter. Something about giving women a voice of their own."

"Oh!" Gwynneth recognized the words she had used. Who would have guessed that Lady Ridgeway would have such a retentive memory.

"I puzzled over why she would repeat herself that way, when she was supposedly trying to keep me from identifying her. I finally decided that, whether she realized it or not, she wanted me to know who she was. Don't you think so, Miss Dunlevvy?" He looked up at her appealingly.

Alarm at his pursuing this line of thought overcame her strong urge to take pity on him. "No, sir, I am sure she did not! Believe me when I say that in no way at all ever does Lady Ridgeway wish to acknowledge the connection." In her agitated eagerness to convince Lord Langley, she tightened the reins sufficiently to irritate even the hardmouthed livery-stable jade she was riding. The mare threw her head up and shook it angrily.

"Easy, Miss Dunlevvy, calm yourself. Even a stable nag can be made to bolt. I shall keep my word. Your . . . our friend shall be as a stranger to me until she makes it very clear that she wishes it otherwise.

The look of relief and gratitude that Gwynneth gave him was so profound that she left him standing there looking somewhat bemused. She urged her feeble mount to hasten, though its pace when cantering was so uneven she felt jolted into a thousand pieces by the time she returned to the livery stables.

When at last she reached her own comfortable parlor, Gwynneth slumped into a chair, limp with relief, to ponder the conversation, the sheer horror of what she had almost let happen. Who would have dreamed Langley would believe that Lady Ridgeway was his mystery correspondent? What would have happened if he had convinced her husband of this would not bear thinking on.

Lord Ridgeway was a rough, domineering, pompous country squire with disdain for the arts and a savage disposition. If he once believed his wife had been the author of letters to Lord Ridgeway, would she have been able to convince him otherwise? Perhaps, when she showed him the letters, he would realize that they were not in his wife's chaotic, cramped hand. But no—that wouldn't have convinced him, for surely he knew his wife hired Gwynneth to act as her amanuensis. This would have seemed merely to confirm his lady's guilt.

And of course the instant this explanation was given, the finger would point to her, if this went any farther. Though she was much more in charity with Lord Langley after his behavior today, she felt more than ever the danger, not just to her precarious social position, but to her tranquility, in having this dynamic, attractive man become aware she was his correspondent. There was quite enough danger in that direction anyway. She had actually hoped he would kiss her today. Gwynneth felt the color flood her face at the memory.

It was madness to be wanting to be kissed by a man who had sworn he would never marry, and who, even if he did marry, would hardly stoop to wed a bookseller.

Feeling somewhat at a loss with her correspondence to Lord Langley in abeyance, she took out a journal in which she intermittently recorded thoughts and drafted poems and essays. The strong emotions of the woodland scene—terror, suspense, relief, admiration, attraction, pressed upon her mind, and it would relieve her to spill her thoughts forth on paper.

Lady Ridgeway surveyed her daughter's toilet with satisfaction. Really, the gel was very well-looking. A country ball or two such as this would give her poise, and she would surely take in London. Of course, there were some prime prospects in Mr. Verleigh's house party, not least of which was the eminently eligible Lord Langley.

Sophisticated—even jaded—and opposed to marriage he might be, but even the most hardened rake had been known, on occasion, to be charmed by an innocent, fresh young beauty. And Lord Langley must marry someday, mustn't he, if he was to have an heir to his title? This pleasant thought brought a smile to Lady Ridgeway's face.

"You will do, my dear," she pronounced, taking Virginia's hand to lead her downstairs.

Lord Langley had to admire Lady Ridgeway's presence, her cool, flawless pretence of scarcely knowing him as she greeted him in the drawing room before dinner. He carefully schooled his own features to be as bland and affable as hers as he bowed over her hand. She presented him to her husband without the slightest hint of trepidation.

Lord Ridgeway was a portly man just above average height, with a big nose and a square, pugnacious jawline. He affected bluff bonhomie as he greeted his guests, but there was that in his eyes and the set of his mouth that suggested a less than agreeable temperament. As Langley stood about, drinking sherry and watching this unlikable man play host, he felt the force of Lady Ridgeway's eloquent request to be allowed to remain anonymous.

At dinner, Langley found himself seated next to Lady Ridgeway, with her nervous, pretty daughter on his other side. Surprised that she would deliberately tempt fate in this way, he nevertheless set himself to make agreeable small talk with both. All through the meal, Lady Regina continued the most convincing imitation of a person just getting acquainted with another person, and Langley managed to avoid the slightest hint that this was not the case.

He felt his reward when she stood to lead the ladies out. The look she gave him was warm and confiding. "Pray do not be too long over your port, Lord Langley. I wish to hear your famous baritone. And my Virginia has an enchanting voice. I know you will exempt her from your famous assertion that 'all sopranos should be drowned.'"

He smiled at her, nodding his head graciously in agreement.

It was over port that Stuart first began to doubt he could keep his bargain, though he saw more than ever the necessity Lady Ridgeway was under of enforcing it.

Lord Ridgeway was, quite simply, detestable. He held forth gleefully on the subject of blood sports, which Langley deplored. He loudly let it be known that he supported the reestablishment of the Bourbon monarchy in France, "even if we have to feed every demmed one of those frogs over the age of ten to the guillotine to make it stick." And when he was well into the bottle, Ridgeway turned to Langley, his small eyes gleaming maliciously in his florid face. "Ain't you the Langley what's encouraging all these women scribblers? Publishing a magazine for 'em, I hear."

Langley agreed that this was so. "Poetry," snorted Ridgeway. "Well, it's a fine waste of everybody's time. Let the ladies read sermons and do needlework, I say! And as for encouraging them to scribble, it's subversive. I'd lock my wife in her room without her dinner if I caught her putting such drivel in print for all to see."

Ridgeway's friends laughed and voiced varying degrees of agreement. Young Dudley ground his teeth and looked as if he would call the man out at any second, and Langley's fury was such that he was for the moment speechless. Nicholas knew his friends' opinions well enough to fear an outbreak of violence, so he attempted to diffuse the situation by observing, "Guess Lady Ridgeway'd have something to say about that."

A few laughs were quickly silenced when the bellicose baron slammed a beefy fist on the table. "I'm the master in my house. Whoever thinks I'm not, lies." He looked belligerently around the table. "Besides," he grumbled, reaching again for the port, "My Regina is a sensible female who thinks as she ought. Riding and seeing to the welfare of her tenants and servants and running her household—that's all she cares about, and that's how it should be."

"And plotting matches for her daughter," Nicholas muttered into Stuart's ear with a grin. Langley forced himself to relax and smile. He made no reply to Lord Ridgeway. He had decided long ago not to waste his energies in contention with the beefeaters, as he designated this kind of unprogressive, dull-witted English type. And certainly it would do his friendship with Lady Ridgeway no good to get into an altercation with her husband. As usual, young Dudley took his cue from Langley, so the tense moment passed away with no explosion.

But to think of his charming, sensitive, thoughtful "Miss Allen" trapped into marriage with such a pig of a man! Langley was more than pleased to leave the men early and join the ladies. So kindly and solicitously did he greet Lady Ridgeway, assuring her he would sing or do anything she commanded, that she blinked and blushed like a maiden.

He ran his eyes tenderly over her face. Yes, she was past forty, and had a few lines to show it, and a few glints of silver, too, in her dark auburn hair. But she was still an attractive woman. She was almost mannish in the vigor of her movements. Outwardly she seemed the perfect mate for her red-faced country baron.

How amazing that she could bring to her poetry such

freshness and innocence, such youthful sensitivity. Had she
written what she had sent him when younger and unmarried, he wondered? And how did she manage to avoid giving way to despair now, yoked as she was to such an
ill-suited mate?

Perhaps he ought to give her some sign of his willingness
to assist her, did she wish to escape the beefeater? But
how?

Chapter Ten

There was time for only a few songs before guests who had not been invited for dinner began to arrive for the ball. In the general movement to the ballroom, Langley was able to ask Lady Ridgeway for a dance. He half expected her to decline, but she calmly agreed, then added, "And I'll trust you to ask my Virginia, too. It's her first grown-up ball, you know."

A very cool head, a very cunning dissembler, he thought as she dealt with him in a sociable, agreeable way, just as she had all through dinner, never by the flicker of an eyelash betraying that either had any deeper knowledge of the other. It was an impressive, almost an unsettling performance, and Langley found himself wondering how long she could keep it up.

He claimed her for the first waltz, which seemed to surprise her a bit, but she accepted without demur. If he thought she would use this slight privacy to acknowledge him, however, he was mistaken. She seized the conversational initiative to voice hopes that he would be in London for her daughter's come-out.

"She's a shy girl, you see. It will mean so much to her to see familiar faces there."

Sardonically he observed, "I am not perhaps the best choice for an entrée into the marriage mart, Lady Ridgeway. I am considered by many to be a walking scandal."

"Because of your ridiculous strictures on marriage, you

mean?" She arched a mobile eyebrow. "Come, Lord Langley. Confess you only speak so to provoke us females."

He laughed heartily. "I've certainly provoked many females in my time. But you've read my views." It was his first chance to allude to their correspondence. "You know I sincerely and deeply believe that marriage enslaves both men and women."

She did not deny knowing of his beliefs, but chuckled indulgently. "Most young bachelors abhor the thought of leg-shackles, Lord Langley. But soon enough a lovely face, a luminous eye, catches them." Her arch manner differed not a whit from that of the dozens of other matchmaking mothers who had belittled his deeply held views on marriage. "Besides, a man such as yourself must needs marry, to produce an heir and secure your title."

"You also know my opinion of titles, my dear." He lowered his voice intimately and looked intently into her brown eyes. "In fact, it is one of the things on which we are in complete agreement."

A look of alarm crossed her face; he could feel her tensing in his arms. "No, no, I don't know of your view of titles. How should I? Don't tell me you are one of these levelers."

What an actress she was! There seemed to be real perplexity in her denial, and real disgust in her attack. Of course, her agitation was caused because he was trying to entice her into admitting their acquaintance. But if he had not known that, he would certainly have been deceived. If she ever did decide to have an affair, her poor husband would be completely fooled by any lie she told him, Langley decided.

"No, then, I won't say it. Rest easy, Lady Ridgeway. I shall say just what you want me to say."

The music was ending. She drew away from him with an uncomfortable look on her face. "I must go and see to my duties as hostess," she said, moving briskly. "I see some young people who are not dancing. Do you come and partner Miss Aimsley, Lord Langley."

Knowing he had trespassed, however slightly, on the boundaries she had set between them, he followed docilely and partnered the young girl presented to him, who was unfortunate enough to have spots but was nevertheless an intelligent, vivacious conversationalist.

Not so Lady Ridgeway's daughter, whom he next addressed. She was indeed a shy girl, and awkward in her shyness, though very pretty with dark auburn hair and her mother's large brown eyes. It was a country-dance, fortunately, so he did not have to exert himself too much in conversing with her.

He was interested to note, as he danced with Miss Ridgeway, that Dudley was dancing with Lady Morley. Since the night that Langley had rejected her, the lovely blond matron had been sending out lures to his young disciple. Now it appeared they were not in vain. Perhaps that would clear the way for Nicholas with Constance Blackwood, that is if John was correct that he had an interest there. These interesting speculations occupied the gaps caused by Miss Ridgeway's conversational deficiencies, but he was glad when the music ended.

As he returned Virginia to her mother, he heard Dudley growl in his ear, "Look who's here."

He turned to see Sir Miles Barlow in animated conversation with Baron Ridgeway. Barlow looked his way, and their eyes locked. There was a challenge in Barlow's expression. "I wonder what progress he is making in his investigation?"

"It looks as if we are about to find out. The snake is heading this way." Dudley rocked back on his heels uneasily.

"We meet again, gentlemen." Sir Miles was at his most urbane. "Lady Ridgeway. Miss Ridgeway." His elaborate bow, hand-kissing ritual, and solicitation for a dance were

all conducted in a manner that suggested he enjoyed knowing he had the attention of a hostile audience. At last, in a
leisurely fashion, he adjusted a faultlessly fitted coat sleeve
and cocked an eyebrow at the two watchful men. "I know
you patriots will be pleased to learn I have made an arrest
in the *Register* case."

Langley's glance flickered to Lady Ridgeway, who was
listening, but her features gave away nothing. "Pray do get
on with telling us, Miles. It is clear you are dying to do so."

"Yes. By all means, Sir Miles. From what my husband
has told me of the affair, this malefactor must be brought to
book immediately." Lady Ridgeway's voice was convincingly indignant.

"I have located a former employee of Mr. Dunlevvy's,
an Irishman, who has been hanging about the area with no
visible means of support. He was one of Dunlevvy's pressmen. Of course, as yet he denies having anything to do with
the posthumous editions of the *Register*, but I feel sure he
will cooperate eventually. Then we shall know who is really behind it." To Langley's consternation, Barlow's
meaningful look was bent on Nicholas Verleigh, just then
dancing by them with Miss Blackwood.

"Stands to reason a poor man must have a rich man to
back him in such an endeavor. As must a poor woman."
Suddenly Barlow's gaze shifted to Langley. "Miss Dunlevvy must have a backer. Someone with radical leanings
and deep pockets."

"Miss Dunlevvy? Ridiculous!" Lady Ridgeway weighed
in vehemently. "That young woman is a lady. From what
Arthur told me, this writing is disgraceful, indecent."

Langley was pleased but by no means surprised by this
defense; Sir Miles was. "What do you know of her, Lady
Ridgeway?"

"I know she is the granddaughter of the Earl of
Fenswicke, and despite her father's eccentric decision to go
into trade, she has always conducted herself decently. She

has in fact made herself very useful to me on more than one occasion. No, Sir Miles, you must look elsewhere for your quarry. Ah, here is Virginia. This next dance is yours, Sir Miles, but I believe my daughter could do with a cooling drink first."

Sir Miles cocked an ironic look at Langley and Dudley before escorting Miss Ridgeway to obtain refreshments. Lady Ridgeway, a determined hostess, then suggested that Dudley and Langley should dance with unpartnered girls.

Just then Nicholas strolled up, Miss Blackwood on his arm. His round face was flushed with exertion and with pleasure. Constance looked extremely pleased with her partner, and barely glanced at Lord Dudley, who seemed undisturbed by this neglect. Instead, he excused himself and sought out Lady Morley again.

Lady Trumbull almost pushed her way through the crowd to reach Miss Blackwood's side. "There you are, my girl. Lord Dudley has been looking everywhere for you. He wishes a dance. You must seek him out and . . ."

"The earl was just here, Aunt, and gave me no indication of pining away for my company." Constance tossed her head and steered Nicholas away.

"Well! Lord Langley, you must assist me. Miss Blackwood's parents will never countenance a match with Mr. Verleigh. They are determined on a match with Lord Dudley."

Langley gave her his most severely depressing stare. "If Miss Blackwood is so foolish as to marry at all, I will be sorry to hear it. But I would be doubly sorry to hear she married a title instead of a man."

On a little whoosh of indignant breath Lady Trumbull turned away, in hot pursuit of her willful niece. John McDougal materialized at Langley's elbow. Obviously he had been listening to this exchange, for he chuckled. "For such a determined dragon, Lady Trumbull is inexplicably ineffective. Nicholas and Constance are smelling of April and May."

"I did not believe you when you told me of his interest, but now I must bow to your superior intuition. But surely he does not mean to marry."

John laughed uneasily. "Pray, Stuart, what else can one do with a respectable lassie one cares deeply for?"

Langley stared down his nose at his Scottish friend repressively. "Even you cannot be so dim as to not know the answer to that question."

"Nay, lad. 'Tis you who are dim, on this subject at least. Fortunately for Miss Blackwood, Nicholas has no such prejudice against parson's mousetrap. With the right bait, he'll enter it most willingly."

"Trap is right. For them both!" Langley strode impatiently away. Talk of marriage usually merely amused him, but for some reason lately it had become an extremely irritating subject.

When he could do so, Langley escaped the hot, overcrowded ballroom for a few minutes of peace and quiet in the Ridgeway's library, where he passed some time in examining the extensive collection.

It was impressive in its scope, though the books all had a rather unused look. Well, naturally that beefeater husband of hers would never touch them! He looked around the elegant, well-appointed room. "Miss Allen" spent many comfortable hours here, reading and writing. A frown creased his forehead as he tried to picture Lady Ridgeway in that role. For some reason, he just couldn't do it.

What a foolish romantic you are, Stuart, he thought. Faced with indisputable evidence to the contrary, you still cling to the concept of Miss Allen as a nubile young female just waiting for you to waken her to love.

He mentally reviewed the evening's experiences. He realized that, however much he might admire Lady Ridgeway's writings, however attuned he might be to her mind, he felt no physical desire for her. She was attractive, but her manner and her style were not such as to engage him.

She had been wise to insist on friendship only, and now he was very glad she had. But he admired her more than ever now, for her spirited and very possibly dangerous defense of Miss Dunlevvy. It strengthened his own determination to assist the young shopkeeper in any way he could, especially as Miles seemed determined somehow to embroil himself and his friends in the venture. In addition to proving her innocence, he might have to prove his own and that of Nicholas and Roger as well.

Chapter Eleven

A thousand little demons of worry pinched and poked at Gwynneth as the day of Lady Ridgeway's ball approached. What would happen there? Would Lord Langley reveal the correspondence, causing havoc with Lady Ridgeway's marriage? Would Lady Ridgeway's behavior make him realize she was not his "Miss Allen?" As they sorted it all out, would Gwynneth herself be unmasked?

To work off some of her anxiety, Gwynneth threw herself into sewing a dress of lavender muslin. She told herself that her decision to begin wearing colors had nothing to do with Lord Langley's compliment on her green riding habit. Rather, his comment had reminded her that her father had also hated the custom of draping women in black for ages after a bereavement. It would actually show more respect for him to wear something more cheerful, she reasoned.

Gwynneth was a competent seamstress, though she disliked sewing. Neatly stitching endless seams she found exceedingly tedious. She especially despised setting the tucks and rouleaux, which were fashionable decorations this year. Yet when Hannah helped her into the dress for a final fitting, just as Lady Ridgeway's guests must be going in to dinner the evening of the ball, she felt such a lift to her fretful spirits that her sewing effort seemed well worth it.

The gown was modish as well as attractive in color, with soft puffed sleeves, a scoop neckline, tucked bodice, high waist, and a long fall of lightly gathered skirt decorated

with two rows of rouleaux near the hemline. As she tightened the ribbon that gave it shape under the bodice, she felt
a little embarrassed at how revealing the style was. Not
only did the dress dip low enough to show her décolleté,
the ribbon fashioned under her bosom seemed to define her
shape sharply. The skirt clung to her figure most sugges-
tively when she moved. Still, she reminded herself as she
turned this way and that to asses the garment in the mirror,
this was what the well dressed were wearing. In fact, it was
more modest than most.

The new dress could not prevent her from experiencing a
nearly sleepless night of worry over what was happening at
the ball. When she finally dozed off she overslept, causing
herself to be late down to the shop on Saturday morning. It
was already open when she peeked around the door to her
office to greet Mr. Highley. To her surprise, he was in conversation with Lord Langley, who immediately stepped
around the corner of the counter and greeted her.

"Ah, Miss Dunlevvy. I was hoping to have a word with
you."

Gwynneth struggled to control her panic. She'd wondered all night what had happened at the ball. Now she
wasn't at all sure that she wanted to know. But it couldn't
be avoided. "Please step in my office, Lord Langley."

Eyes twinkling mischievously, he seized her hands and
drew her forward. "No indeed, Miss Dunlevvy. Mr. Highley and I are agreed that you are in this dark office too
much. I have brought my curricle. Please ride out with me.
It is a very pleasant day."

Gwynneth could see that it was. Her hands tingled where
he held them, and that was pleasant, too. Entirely too pleasant. "I thank you, my lord, but I cannot."

"Now, Miss Gwynny . . ."

She gave Highley a quelling look. "Ezekial! You know
how the biddies would tear me apart if they saw me driving
out unaccompanied with Lord Langley or any other man."

"But we shan't be unaccompanied, Miss Dunlevvy. I've brought my tiger, see. All the proprieties shall be observed, I assure you."

Gwynneth peered out the windows, torn between awareness of how dangerous association with this man could be, and longing to experience a drive behind those handsome grays she could see champing at their bits. "Well . . ."

"Fetch your bonnet, my dear, and hurry. Mustn't keep Lord Langley's fine cattle standing." She looked up into Mr. Highley's thin, lined face and saw his kindly determination that she have this treat.

"Very well." Gwynneth dashed upstairs and hurriedly checked her hair in the mirror before donning an old but still attractive chip-straw bonnet. How fortunate that she had worn her new lavender dress this morning! She pinched her cheeks to bring the color, then stopped and stared at her image in the mirror as Hannah stood behind her, full of disapproval.

"No good will come of going about with these gent'men, Miss Gwynny. Thought you'd learned that lesson."

"You are right, Hannah. Well, I've accepted his invitation now, but I'll make sure he does not leave the town."

"Mind you do."

Gwynneth walked slowly downstairs. She mustn't let Lord Langley see her looking as eager and excited as she had a moment ago. It wouldn't do to encourage him to take any special notice of her, since she knew his intentions could hardly fail to be dishonorable.

How wary the chit looks, and no wonder, Langley thought as he led her out to his waiting curricle. Our first meeting must be very much on her mind. Once again he cursed himself for the ill-advised attempt to kiss her.

Determined to put her at her ease, he immediately began talking about Lady Ridgeway. "I simply had to talk to someone about last night, and you are the only one who understands the situation."

"Lord Langley, be careful. Your tiger will hear . . ."

"I shall be careful; only you will know to whom I refer. At any rate, Edward is very discreet. He has served me for years and never betrayed a confidence yet."

Gwynneth felt her cheeks pinking up a little at the thought of the kinds of things Edward might have had to exercise his discretion over.

Mistaking her emotion, Langley hastened to assure her, "Don't look so anxious, Miss Dunlevvy. I didn't disgrace or embarrass your friend last night. I was discretion itself. No one would ever guess that she and I had been corresponding for three years. In fact, I could scarce believe it myself."

"Wh-what do you mean?"

"She should go upon the stage. Or be a diplomat. A spy, even. She could do anything requiring a cool head and the ability to dissemble, to appear completely calm. You know she must have had some trepidation, yet—oh, she was magnificent."

Gwynneth looked at his enthusiastic expression and felt a jolt of guilt, not the first she'd felt since letting him think Lady Ridgeway was Miss Allen. Oddly enough, she also felt a little envy that his good opinion was not directed toward her.

"But I was magnificent, too. You would surely have been proud of me. Only one lapse, while we were waltzing."

Gwynneth drew in her breath sharply. This was the fear that had kept her tossing and turning all night long—that he and Lady Ridgeway would find a chance for a private tête-à-tête. But Lord Langley rushed on. "I attempted to allude to things she could only know about through our correspondence, and she put me off right away. You would have thought she was genuinely surprised and puzzled by what I said."

"What . . . what were you discussing?"

"Marriage, and my feelings about titles."

From their correspondence, Gwynneth knew very well his views on both marriage and titles, and he knew hers, but she feared to enter a substantive conversation with him, for she might betray herself by her opinions or her phraseology. So she contented herself with a bland "Oh?"

"Yes. She ripped up at me, said she hoped I wasn't a leveler. She who has agreed with me that a titled, inherited aristocracy is an anachronism."

His face settled into a frown, and he stared out at the fields they were slowly passing for a moment. "Much as I admire her acting ability, I also admit to a little uneasiness. So accomplished a dissembler. Who would ever know whether to believe her in anything, once he had seen such a performance? Do you think it bespeaks a moral flaw?"

It was Gwynneth's turn to frown, guilt assailing her again. How could she agree to attribute to Lady Ridgeway a moral flaw of which she was innocent. "No-o-o. I think she has to consider her husband . . . that is, it is a wife's duty . . . umm . . ."

Langley broke in upon her stammering. "Yes, yes, that beast of a husband. I mustn't lose sight for a moment of him in judging her character. He is truly a despicable man. Of course she must exercise every caution in dealing with such a creature."

Here Gwynneth felt on safer ground. She had never liked Lord Ridgeway herself. He seemed to her to combine all the worst flaws of the landed aristocracy with none of their virtues. Doubtless Lord Langley would be horrified to know that Lady Ridgeway was quite fond of her liege lord, though she often circumvented his narrow strictures, mostly in her daughters' interests.

So she didn't hesitate to assent to his opinion. "I agree. He is truly unpleasant. How she can bear him I do not know."

"Nor I." Lord Langley seemed much stricken by her

comment. "If I had the faintest hint she wished it, I would help her escape from him. Such a noble spirit, to be linked with such common clay!"

Gwynneth watched his long, serious face in fascination as it took on a fierce look, nostrils flaring. What a passionate, mercurial temperament he had. He reminded her of a high-blooded stallion, mettlesome, proud, strong, but excitable and difficult to control. Almost instinctively she began to speak to him as she would to such an animal, in a low, soothing voice.

"You mustn't, Lord Langley. She is very well-off, I assure you. For all his bluster, I've never seen him mistreat her. Indeed, she is not a low-spirited creature. She stands her ground with him, and I believe is truly fond of him."

"Fond! How could she be?"

Gwynneth was on solid ground here. "What draws two people together is sometimes mysterious, Lord Langley, but I assure you, she has always seemed contented with him since I have known them. They share many interests, such as their love of fine horses. She is proud of his family connections, and is a very involved mother, as you know."

"Yes, I saw that. Her concern for her daughter is touching. Though you'd think, knowing me as she does, she'd not put the child in my way, wouldn't you, Miss Dunlevvy?"

"Perhaps she doesn't take all your pronouncements against marriage seriously, Lord Langley."

"Indeed she does not, but she should. Why, her own condition is prima facie evidence against the institution. Yoked to a man who swears he'd lock his wife in her room if she published poetry, how else could she behave in our society but to hide that part of herself, to dissemble—in fact, to live a lie."

As it was Gwynneth who was "living a lie" just then, she was once more struck dumb. They drove on in silence for quite a spell.

The wind flowed past her face with sibilant seductiveness, and she lifted her head to it. How cool and pleasant it felt on this warm day. She hadn't been in a curricle like this for years, not since Charles . . .

"Enjoying yourself?"

She turned to see Lord Langley's gaze resting on her, a half smile on his face, the expression in his dark eyes almost tender.

"Very much! Such a beautiful day. And the view up here is lovely. I . . . oh, gracious!"

"What is the matter, Miss Dunlevvy?"

"I had not intended to leave town with you. That is, I . . ." She had been so involved in their conversation that she had entirely lost track of where they were.

"Am I forever in your black books because of our first meeting, my dear? Can you not trust me now?"

"I would like to think so, but . . ."

"Then do. Should you like to drive my team?"

Gwynneth was instantly diverted. Even when they were almost engaged, Charles Osgood would never have dreamed of letting her touch his horses' reins. "You would let me? I am vastly flattered." Gwynneth considered where they were. Lord Langley had steered them up into the hills to the southwest of Guilford. They were near the top of a fairly steep rise, and the road, actually little more than a path, was narrow.

"I think I had better not try just now. I've never driven a team before. Perhaps I'll just relax and enjoy the drive, thank you."

"Excellent. The view from this rise is exquisite. The one superiority I can concede to this part of England is its many exquisite views."

"Where . . . where are we going?" She had become intensely aware of the masculine appeal of the man beside her all of a sudden.

"I had no destination in mind. I just wanted someone to

talk to. You've been a good listener, for which I thank you."

Gwynneth flushed, again guiltily conscious of her true role, and said nothing.

"I expect it is a great comfort to . . . ah, to our friend, to have a confidante."

"Really, Lord Langley, I don't want to give you a false impression. I'm not so very close to her."

"You've read her letters to me?"

"Well . . . some of them."

"And she's shown you at least some of mine."

"I . . . ah, yes, a few."

"I would say you are a very trusted confidante. Considering that husband of hers, she has put the means to destroy her in your hands."

"Oh, I would never . . ."

"Of course you wouldn't." His eyes were warm with approval. "And she showed last night that she not only appreciates but returns your loyalty."

"What do you mean?"

"That snake Barlow was at the ball. He has arrested a former employee of your father's as a possible suspect in the case of the posthumous issues of the *Register*. He insinuated that you were involved, and she informed him quite firmly that that was impossible!"

Gwynneth felt a flush of real warmth for Lady Ridgeway for the first time. She had worked for the woman, and appreciated her good qualities, but had never really liked her until now. "That was very good of her. I am distressed to hear that Sir Miles still suspects me. I wonder why?"

"Sir Miles suspects everyone who isn't an arch-Tory. Try not to worry about it. Nicholas and I are keeping our ears open. We'll stand your friend if he tries to arrest you."

Gwynneth suppressed a shudder. "How terrible. I expected he would have dropped his suspicions by now. I know I am innocent, so I felt it must be obvious."

"It will become obvious to him, I promise you." Seeing the expression of distress on her face, Langley set himself to distract her and rechannel the conversation. "Tell me. Do you discuss books with Lady Ridgeway? Does she read you her poetry?"

Gwynneth thought of the hours she'd spent cutting books for Lady Ridgeway, and of the summaries she always gave of them, to save the lady the trouble of reading them herself.

"Yes, we do discuss books, extensively, but . . ." Oh, this was intolerable, all this lying. She had to end it; she was miserable at so much dishonesty. "I think I'd best be getting back."

"You don't like to talk about her, do you?" His look was shrewd.

"I just wouldn't want to accidentally violate a confidence."

"Well, I doubt that's possible, but I admire your scruples." They had for some moments been stopped at the crest of the hill, looking out over the panoramic folds of the landscape spread below them. In the foreground Guilford's roofs and church spires shone in the bright sun. "Shall we continue on this road? It connects with the London road back to Guilford about a mile hence?" Gwynneth nodded her head, and Langley clicked at his horses, which was all the office they needed to move forward.

"So, let us discuss you, Miss Dunlevvy."

"Me? No, I . . . I'm not very interesting."

"I think you are. A young girl . . ."

"I am one and twenty, sir!"

"Ah, forgive me, a young woman, then, running a profitable bookstore by herself. An earl's granddaughter, living entirely independently. Rather unusual."

"Not my choice, I assure you. If only the shop *were* profitable—I'd sell it in a minute."

"Would you? Why? I suppose you wish to get away from

trade?" His voice sounded disapproving, as if there was something cowardly in such a desire.

Gwynneth frowned. "Being in trade has become a bitter exile for me, sir. Can you not understand that?"

"Then what would you do, when you've sold out? Purchase a husband?"

Gwynneth allowed herself a cynical laugh. "Marriage does not form part of my plans."

Amazed, Langley almost dropped the reins. "I thought every young girl dreamed of marriage." His eyes probed her features with new interest.

"Oh, I do *dream* of marriage, Lord Langley. But I no longer expect it in reality."

"Why not, may I ask? Not that I would encourage a woman to enslave herself, but you seem in no way unsuited to marriage to me."

"I thank you for that, but not all the gentry hold your democratical views, my lord. The man I had thought I would marry spent an entire afternoon about a year ago convincing me just how unmarriageable I am."

"This would be Charles Osgood, I collect."

"How did you . . . ? Never mind. I know scandal is served with tea in our small hamlet as well as in London salons. Yes, Charles, who stood by me so admirably, or so I thought, when my father's descent into trade caused me to be snubbed by most of those who once called themselves my friends."

"Oh, this damnable English snobbery. 'Tis out of all reason that a lovely, well-bred female should be cut because her father owns a bookstore. Indeed, you ought to be able to continue to own it yourself, get your living by it, and be accepted wherever you go."

"My, you are a utopian, sir." She smiled at him. "But I am painfully aware of how the class from which I come regards me. Ch-Charles made that all too clear."

The memory that assailed her brought tears to her eyes.

Langley used his free hand to tilt her chin up and study her. "There's more to this than just a broken promise, isn't there?"

Why she felt she could confide in him, she wasn't sure. She hadn't even told her father the truth about her last interview with Charles. But the grave face, the deep brown eyes now so gently looking into her own, encouraged her. "Yes. Much more. He . . . he explained that his father now objected to our marriage, but he assured me we'd be together always. He kissed me as he never had before, and asked me to come away with him. He told me I'd have a nice cottage in the country, and when he went up to the city, I'd have a fine little house there, with my own carriage. Words cannot adequately convey my pain when it gradually dawned on me that what I would not have was his name."

Langley swore softly under his breath. "Spineless!"

"He begged me to accept. He swore he loved me, that he could not live without me. But when I still refused, he returned home and announced his engagement. Shortly thereafter he married Evangaline Beauchamps, once one of my very best friends and the first to cut me when my father opened the bookstore."

"I regret your having been hurt, Miss Dunlevvy, but perhaps you are better off as it is. I quite wonder at young girls running into marriage as they do, when it is a legal form of slavery, after all is said and done."

"Your . . . your views on marriage are known to me, Lord Langley. But I suspect you cannot have thought carefully about the consequences for young women who would follow your program. They would be viewed as cyprians, as mistresses. I could never do such a thing. After all, if I hurt by being ostracized merely for being a bookseller, think how painful it would be to be treated as a whore."

He covered her hands, which were clinched tightly in her lap, with his in a soothing gesture. "I do understand. Until the laws and society's attitudes are changed, it would take a brave woman to disdain marriage. And these practical objections are the most telling ones. Morality is but a thin cover for practicality."

"That is not at all how I feel." She jerked her hands free. "You don't know me at all. I could never live in sin, no matter if you could guarantee me complete and utter social acceptance."

He drew back and gave her an amused look. "Since I certainly couldn't guarantee that, we'll never be able to test that proposition. Don't fly up into the boughs. I am sure that you are all that is respectable—ah, moral."

He was laughing at her. Exasperated, Gwynneth turned away from him. This intense conversation had kept her from noticing they'd returned to town. She held her tongue, though she wanted to give him a strong dressing down, because she didn't want to be seen arguing with him as they drove through the streets.

He pulled up in front of her shop and tossed the reins to his tiger. Gwynneth tried to get down before he could come around to help her, but he was too quick. When he set her on the pavement, his hands lingered on her waist. "A pity you have so many, umm, scruples, Miss Dunlevvy. You are a very pleasant armful." A diabolical grin lit his features.

She tried to slap him, but he intercepted her wrist in midair. "None of that. Remember the last time you came to cuffs with me, Miss Dunlevvy?" His eyes danced with glee at her consternation. "Or perhaps you would like for me to kiss you right here on the street?"

Furious, Gwynneth jerked out of his arms and raced to the door of the shop. He caught up to her in one stride and turned her around with a firm hand on her elbow.

"Come, let us cry friends. I was only teasing you a bit to jog you out of your blue devils. Your virtue is safe with me, Miss Dunlevvy. I value too much having someone to talk to about Lady Ridgeway."

Gold eyes locked with brown, and Langley found himself holding his breath, and wondering if he was a liar, for truly, this pretty bookseller made his blood run hot. As for Gwynneth, she felt again that surge of desire that told herself she'd best get far away from this exciting man or she'd betray every scruple she'd ever had.

So she forced herself to smile. "Of course we may cry friends." She held out her hand for a brief handshake. "Thank you for the drive. I enjoyed it." Primly she drew herself up and hurried into her shop, away from what she very much feared was his knowing scrutiny. She doubted she had fooled him with her primness. The man knew his powers of attraction!

So occupied with her thoughts was she that she didn't see Sir Miles Barlow until she careened straight into him.

Chapter Twelve

Blinded by the contrast between the bright sunlight she had just come from and the dark bookshop, Gwynneth did not see Sir Miles Barlow waiting for her just inside the door. She hit him with such force that her bonnet flew off and her flyaway hair slipped its pins and tumbled about her shoulders.

"From Lord Langley's arms into mine in less than a moment. What an amiable chit you are to be sure, Miss Dunlevvy." Instead of steadying her on her feet, Sir Miles held her closely, wrapping his arms around her and meeting her shocked golden-hazel eyes with his insinuating gaze. "Dare I hope that you prefer mine to his?"

"I would prefer not to be mauled by either of you, sir." Gwynneth jerked free of his grasp and pushed past him. Mr. Highley had already uttered a protest and started across the room toward them.

"You will treat Miss Dunlevvy with respect, sir, or I will . . ."

Barlow waived a dismissive hand toward the agitated clerk. "I will treat Miss Dunlevvy just as she ought to be treated. I must have a word with you, my dear. In private." He grasped Gwynneth's arm and steered her toward her office door.

Cheeks flaming, Gwynneth was deeply grateful that the shop was empty of customers at the time. "Unhand me!

Whatever you need to say to me may be said in front of Mr. Highley."

"Hoity-toity. You shouldn't take that tone with me, Miss Dunlevvy. I am a man whose goodwill you should cultivate. Perhaps you will be more accommodating when you learn that I have arrested one Ian Mulhenny."

Jerking her arm free, Gwynneth stepped back and met her tormentor's eyes steadily. "What has that to do with me."

"Surely you aren't going to pretend you know nothing of the man?"

"I know that he worked as a printer for my father, and that I had the unpleasant task of letting him go after my father fell ill."

"That is not the tale he tells."

"Then he lies, sir." Highley ranged himself at Gwynneth's side. "I was present when she dismissed him. A rare dustup it was. He expected her to continue to print the paper, and when she tried to explain she had no money to pay him or the other print-shop workers, he accused her of lying. He was most disrespectful. I had to evict him forcibly from the premises."

"What is your name, my man?" Sir Miles turned a menacing face to the clerk, withdrawing a small notebook from his pocket.

"Ezekial Highley, sir."

"Then I should tell you, Mr. Highley, that you are taking a great risk in inserting yourself into an investigation into libel and sedition against our prince and his government."

"I knew nothing of sedition or libel, and neither does Miss Dunlevvy." Mr. Highley stood his ground. Gwynneth had begun to tremble, whether in fear or rage, she knew not which.

"Surely you don't still suspect me of publishing that scurrilous paper, Sir Miles? Your investigation of the press and typeface must have proven to you that . . ."

"That the posthumous issues of the *Register* were indeed printed on none other than your printing press, Miss Dunlevvy. Ah, how well you do surprise, my dear."

"Impossible. That place has been shut up since her father took sick. And she didn't even know where the keys were, if you will remember."

"Or so she pretended." Barlow turned his back on Mr. Highley, confronting Gwynneth directly. "The paper was printed on your press. The irregularities and peculiarities of your type are identical to those of the recent issues of the *Register*." Sir Miles smiled at Gwynneth's white face. "Perhaps now you will consent to talk to me privately, my sweet? After all, Newgate is no place for the virtuous, but I am told that no woman is virtuous in Newgate for long."

"I am innocent of any wrongdoing."

"That is what I am hoping to give you a chance to do—convince me of your innocence." The leer he gave her left little doubt as to how he hoped to be convinced.

Gwynneth had to throw herself in front of the intrepid Mr. Highley, who appeared about to attack the baronet. "My innocence can be established without private interviews with you, sir. I mean to engage counsel, and I should warn you that I am not without friends."

"Yes, I just saw you with one of your 'friends,' didn't I. But let me warn you, Miss Dunlevvy. You would do better to trust yourself to my protection than Lord Langley's, for he is under suspicion, too, and may well have all he can manage to save himself."

"As for 'protection' in that nasty intonation that you give it, I accept that from no man. I have friends, many friends, here in this country, and will seek legal advice forthwith. My innocence is all the protection I need."

"Deliciously naive, or artful, I cannot decide just which." Barlow's snide smile belied his assertion of perplexity. "We will have more delightful conversations of this nature. And perhaps Mr. Highley may be questioned, too. I am sure the jail here in Guilford will hold him as well as his accomplice Mr. Mulhenny."

"If you think to intimidate me, sir . . ."

"I think to warn you."

"You will not succeed. I know nothing of the publication of this paper, no more than Miss Dunlevvy does, but I know a rum bit of blackmail when I see it, and I suggest you leave now!"

Seeing that the unprepossessing middle-aged clerk showed no signs of being intimidated, Sir Miles bowed urbanely, though his fury at being thwarted showed in his tense face. "I shall leave, but neither of you have heard the last of this." Turning calmly, he sauntered out of the shop, leaving two very shaken people behind.

"Oh, Miss Gwynny, here's a coil. Will Lord Langley really stand your friend? For that one's a dirty dish, make no mistake. I very much fear you are in danger."

"Lord Langley pledged himself to aid me, and also Mr. Verleigh, whose word weighs most heavily with the local magistrate."

Since Mr. Verleigh *was* the local magistrate, Highley stared at her for a moment and then chuckled. "How you can joke at this moment, miss!"

A smile quirked her mouth, but Gwynneth's eyes were serious. "You are right, of course. It is not a joke, and not a local matter, either. Lord Langley mentioned my seeking legal advice. I wonder if he can make a recommendation? A local solicitor may not be what I need. I will send a note to him, asking him to suggest someone. Thank you for standing by me, Ezekial. I fear you have made trouble for yourself by doing so."

"Never you mind about that. Promised your father I'd look after you, and so I will." Highley patted the hand that she had laid on his arm. "You look quite done in, Miss Gwynny. Why don't you go on upstairs and let Hannah fix you a nice tea. Can't do anything about a lawyer till Monday anyway, I don't suppose."

Gwynneth stood irresolute for a moment. Her knees were trembling with delayed reaction, so that she wasn't sure she could climb the stairs, but tea sounded so soothing just now—tea and Hannah's comforting presence.

"Thank you, Ezekial. If you will lock up, I believe I will do just that. I'll pen the note tonight, and send it over to Lord Langley tomorrow."

"Excellent notion, miss. I'll see to everything."

Gwynneth wearily tossed on her pillows that night, unable to sleep. She hardly knew which problem worried her more, the situation with Lord Langley, or the danger of being charged with libel and treason by Sir Miles Barlow. The latter seemed so absurd to her that she was inclined to dismiss it as an empty charge by a rake hoping to coerce her into his bed.

Between the danger of being coerced into his bed or coaxed into Lord Langley's, she felt the greater danger lay with any continued association with the handsome baron. And yet, she must needs ask him for help against Sir Barlow, just in case the man was as ruthless as he pretended. It was, as Highley said, a coil.

Taking care to disguise her handwriting, she had sent Langley a note to which he immediately replied. His familiar hasty scrawl informed her that he would write to London forthwith, requesting the assistance of a barrister experienced in just these kinds of cases.

Her mind considerably eased, Gwynneth attended evening services and then turned her attention to letting out and retrimming the bodice of her riding habit, though she wasn't at all sure why, as she had no immediate prospects of riding again.

The following day Gwynneth suffered a new addition to her worries when Lady Ridgeway arrived. Mr. Highley announced her as if he were a butler, giving his employer a wink as he did so, and the imperious matron sailed into her office, her daughter Virginia in her wake.

"Miss Dunlevvy! Do you know Lord Langley?"

"I, ah, know who he is, of course. He has come in here to purchase . . ."

"Yes, yes. You are familiar with his writing, his publications, I mean?"

"Oh, yes. Lord Langley is well-known for . . ."

"Good. I want you to take Virginia in hand, tell her all about him, what she must read to be knowledgeable about his interests."

"Well, Lady Ridgeway, I'll be glad to do it if you wish, but I think you should know Lord Langley has interests and views which many see as quite scandalous and entirely unsuitable for a young, unmarried girl to know."

The usually imperturbable matron looked troubled. "He hinted at some such to me Friday night. But surely it's all just the usual rebelliousness of a young pup. Outgrow it in time."

"Perhaps, but . . ." Did Lady Ridgeway not realize the "young pup" was thirty-two?

"Mean to say, she's got to have something to talk to him about. Gel gets completely tongue-tied around him."

Gwynneth turned to Virginia. "So you've set your cap for the wicked Lord Langley?"

Virginia turned quite purple with embarrassment. "He's very handsome, isn't he?"

Gwynneth sighed. The girl was a willing party to Lady Ridgeway's matrimonial schemes. But any further entanglement of herself with the Ridgeways and Lord Langley enhanced her chance of discovery. Not to mention the fact that some of Langley's notions about love and marriage might well do harm to a young girl without firm principles.

"Well," Lady Ridgeway harrumphed. "Can you help us?"

"If this is truly what you want, my lady. He is very fond

of poetry of all sorts and patronizes writers of both sexes. I don't suppose you write any poetry yourself?" She turned to the young girl watching her so expectantly.

"No," Virginia shook her head.

"Do you read it?"

"No." The girl hung her head a little. "I don't read much at all. My father prefers me to read sermons and improving works, and it's all such a bore so I just . . . don't read."

"That's it, then." The words popped out of her mouth without her thinking, and both women looked at her expectantly. Immediately Gwynneth wished she hadn't said anything, but now she must go on.

"You tell him how deprived you've been by your father's attitude. Lord Langley is also a very strong advocate of women being well educated, you see."

By their puzzled frowns, Gwynneth realized that neither Virginia nor her mother did see.

"So you ask his advice. Ask him to tell you if he thinks women should be educated. He'll expound on that, I'm sure." Gwynneth felt a strong sense of revulsion at the trap she was helping to lay, a trap that might be very effective. She realized that she didn't want it to succeed. Still, she was too far in to back out now.

"Then you should agree with him and ask what he would recommend for you to read. Your mother has quite a good library."

"Might work, Miss Dunlevvy," Lady Ridgeway broke in. "We'll call on Mr. Verleigh today, see if she can get a word with Langley."

"But, Lady Ridgeway, what if he suggests she read something scandalous or inappropriate?"

"She don't have to read it. Like as not you will have. You can tell her in general what it's about, and what she should object to."

Gwynneth was none too happy with this assignment, nor with the determined woman's assumption that she was familiar with scandalous literature. "Really, Lady Ridgeway, I don't . . ."

"Tut, tut, girl. Pay you for your time. Good customer of yours when most wouldn't patronize that flaming radical of a father of yours, wasn't I? What's more, when that mincing fool Miles Barlow hinted you were publishing a treasonous newspaper, didn't I set him straight?"

"Oh, you don't have to pay me. I'm very grateful for all you have done for me."

"Yes, and so you should be. Well, I'm grateful to you, too. You're clever. I've recognized that all along. Been very helpful to me. And this idea of yours is a good one. We'll put it in train immediately." Lady Ridgeway sailed majestically out, her smiling daughter trailing behind.

Here was another nasty coil! Gwynneth felt a shudder of apprehension. She was getting in worse and worse—and now Virginia was naively going to throw herself at a man who appeared to lack either any sense of propriety or scruples. She would feel herself to be partially to blame if the ploy caught his interest, or brought harm to the young girl.

The thought of Virginia and Lord Langley together sent an unexpected jolt of distaste through Gwynneth. It took her a while to recognize the emotion, and then she tried to deny it. She couldn't be! But she was. She was jealous.

Heavens! What was wrong with her. The man was a disaster. She surely couldn't be wanting his dangerous attentions. But she found herself fiercely resentful that Virginia could go to Mr. Verleigh's, meet Langley on terms of social equality, walk with him, go riding with him, flirt with him. And she, Gwynneth Dunlevvy, could do nothing but sit in her shop, ordering books, inventorying books, and counting receipts.

It made her almost as miserable as she'd been when Charles had broken off their understanding, offering her carte blanche instead. As nothing else had done, that had made her aware of the gulf her father's entering trade had opened between herself and her former social equals. Now she felt again the sense of being shut out that had, at times, made her unfairly angry with her beloved father.

To combat these lowering reflections, she threw herself into the stitching of another dress. She had purchased lengths of cloth for several garments, and consulted *La Belle Assemblee* and *The Ladies' Magazine* carefully before cutting them. This one was of spring-green crepe de chine, and she daringly made it in the new shorter skirt length now in vogue. The scalloped hem would show off Gwynneth's trim ankles. She had even ordered some dainty slippers dyed to match. The luxurious material, low neckline, and figure-skimming drapery would make the dress suitable for evening wear, though where and when she would have occasion to wear it, she couldn't imagine.

It will be perfect for those evenings at the theater in London, she thought. Then laughed at her own folly. By the time she could carry out her plans and get to London, doubtless this dress would be sadly out of date. But the woman in her had craved the green silk, and felt well rewarded when she first slipped it on for a trial fitting.

Hannah's seamed face lit up, and she sighed with pleasure as she twitched the garment into place. " 'Tis a perfect fit, Miss Gwynny. And it shows your figure a treat!"

Gwynneth's mirror told her Hannah did not exaggerate. A glow of color washed her cheeks as she fingered the neckline. "Thank you, Hannah, but don't you think the neckline is a little too . . . ?"

"Not no more nor those in the fancy books," Hannah asserted loyally.

"And the color. Perhaps it is too soon for this color, but . . ."

Hannah knew when her beloved nursling needed reassurance. " 'Tis a lovely color, Miss Gwynny. It is a true pleasure to see you out of the black. And you know what your father would have wanted."

"You do think Papa would approve?"

"That he would, miss. He hated mourning clothes so. Said we ought to celebrate if we really believed, you know."

"I know." Tears came to her eyes as Gwynneth remembered how her father had comforted her as he was dying.

"Don't weep for me, Gwynneth, unless they be tears of joy, my dear. I'm passing out of this dull place into a larger, finer life beyond." He had dried her tears as almost his last act before death claimed him.

Gwynneth fell into a deep abstraction, thinking of how much she missed her sometimes feckless but always loving and vibrant father. At last Hannah recalled her to her task by fussing with the hemline of her dress.

"I think I will make a lace collar in white or blonde to wear with this, though. It is a little too . . . décolleté for any need I have."

Hannah shook her head. "You will need it, Miss Gwynny. I know you will. You won't remain forever in this bookshop."

"Thank you, Hannah." Gwynneth gave her a quick hug. "Now let us decide how to cut the violet tulle." She immersed herself in the sewing project, thus keeping at bay her fears about two very different but very dangerous men.

Chapter Thirteen

On Wednesday, Lord Langley appeared once more at Gwynneth's door. As she was upstairs, sewing, she flushed with surprise and embarrassment when Hannah opened the door to admit him. As she rose to greet him, the green silk she was working on slithered out of her hand.

"Forgive the intrusion, Miss Dunlevvy. I told Mr. Highley I must see you, and he was busy in the shop so I just came up." Lord Langley's eyes beamed with approval as he beheld her startled face, her shapely pink mouth in a small "O" of surprise. "Did I tell you the other day that lavender makes those elusive eyes look almost green?" His comprehensive survey seemed to take in a great deal more than just the fact that she was once again wearing her new dress. He bent and lifted the silk. "And this color will be *ravissante* on you," he murmured, holding it up to her face and letting the soft fabric caress her skin.

Gwynneth felt the heat of a blush on her cheek. Indeed, it seemed as if her entire body was suddenly afire. Her emotions were only heightened by noticing how he seemed to dwarf her small parlor, his muscular shoulders and long legs loudly proclaiming his masculinity.

She quickly covered her embarrassment with social graces, offering her visitor a chair and tea. She chattered nervously to hide her astonishment, embarrassment, and, yes, intense pleasure, in seeing him.

As he settled into her father's favorite chair, she reflected painfully on the poverty of her surroundings compared to what he was surely accustomed to. They had sold most of her mother's expensive furniture to raise capital for her father's business venture. It has been replaced with plain, serviceable pieces of local manufacture. She had all the necessities of life, but few of the luxuries a man like Lord Langley would expect.

Yet he seemed entirely at ease in these humble surroundings. His manner was agreeably different from the shock and pity that Charles had displayed upon finding himself in this small shopkeeper's parlor.

When an obviously disapproving Hannah had laid out the tea and retreated from the room, leaving the door to the kitchen open for propriety's sake, Lord Langley launched into his reason for being there without further ado.

"I had to turn to your sympathetic and understanding ear again, Miss Dunlevvy. I hope you won't mind too much. You'll never guess what has happened."

Gwynneth grasped her cup tightly, her eyes wide on his. "What?" She managed to croak.

"Oh, don't look so distressed. Lady Ridgeway is not unmasked before her liege lord or anything so dramatic as that. But Virginia, her daughter, has made a dead set at me, with her mother's connivance. It seems my 'Miss Allen' wants me for a son-in-law."

"And what . . . that is, do you . . . ?" Gwynneth stumbled over her words.

"My views on marriage remain unchanged, even with the prospect of such a *desirable* connection." He gave her a roguish smile and a wink. "A weary life sentence of slavery and misery! And particularly with an empty head like Miss Ridgeway's. If ever I were so mad as to become leg-shackled, it would certainly be to a very different type of woman."

"It must be embarrassing for you, then."

"Yes, deucedly. The chit is clearly enamored of me—

wearing her heart on her sleeve. And a man must be so careful around these innocent young girls. The slightest misstep and he's said to have compromised them. Though they'd catch cold at trying to snare me that way, I wouldn't want to do the child an injury. Not even if she weren't Lady Ridgeway's daughter."

Gwynneth felt a surge of pleasure to hear him voice these very proper sentiments. "So you are not quite the unprincipled rake you are reputed to be." She bit her lower lip in chagrin at her unpremeditated plain speaking.

Instantly he looked troubled, offended. "It seems people *must* misunderstand me. Perhaps it is a way of not seeing the sense in what I say. I shun marriage as much because of the harm it does to women as from any inclination to wantonness. I would never knowingly hurt an innocent girl, of whatever class, for a casual affair. Our sex has much to answer for! I am not a rake and never have been. Any liaisons I have formed have been with women of the world who . . ."

"Please, Lord Langley," Gwynneth murmered. Her cheeks were quite scarlet.

"Forgive me. I forget you are only slightly older and hardly more experienced than Miss Ridgeway. I shouldn't say my confessions to you." The heavy eyebrows drew together, the deep brown eyes pleaded forgiveness.

It flustered and enchanted Gwynneth to see that he looked genuinely contrite.

"It's just that you seem somehow very, ah, how can I word it? Solid, in your understanding. I don't know how I know, I just feel it. But I won't embarrass you further. It's simply that something about this has me rather agitated, even a bit disillusioned, as regards our mutual friend. I wanted to see if you could . . . oh, I suppose I'm hoping you can dispel my doubts." He ran large hands through his thick hair in agitation.

Gwynneth's heart beat loudly at the word "doubts." Was

he beginning to suspect? But she managed to keep a composed countenance, lifting her eyebrows encouragingly as he hesitated.

"You see, Miss Dunlevvy, Monday afternoon Lady Ridgeway and Miss Ridgeway called on Nicholas and somehow maneuvered me into escorting the daughter through the rose garden. There she confessed in low tones her interest in my views on women's education. She begged me for advice on what she should read to become better educated, as she knew herself to be sadly deficient."

"For many women, Lord Langley, what passes for education is little more than reading, writing, and sewing, with deportment and dancing thrown in."

"Yes, and apparently that is very much the case with Miss Ridgeway. I quizzed her a bit, to see what education she has received, and I was appalled. Why, do you know she hasn't even read any Shakespeare? She says her father wants her to read only sermons and improving literature. But perhaps you, a vicar's daughter after all, have been similarly raised?"

"No, Lord Langley. My father agreed with Mary Wollstonecraft that women are rational creatures whose minds can be, must be, improved by education. He taught me himself, and encouraged me to learn as much as I would. It is difficult to imagine Lord Ridgeway's attitude."

"Indeed! Poor child. I gave her a few hints, and asked how she would manage to get books if her father objected."

"What did she say," Gwynneth asked, wondering how the ingenious Virginia had gotten past this hurdle.

"Artless creature. She said if I recommend them, her mother would let her get them from the library, as her mother hoped . . . here she blushed and looked most charmingly confused, and I had to burst out laughing."

He laughed richly at the memory, and Gwynneth smiled, enjoying the sight of his head tilted back to expose the strong column of his throat.

Then he underwent one of those mercurial changes of moods she had observed before. His long face took on an almost angry seriousness, and he sat his cup down with a frown. The dark eyes he raised to her were troubled.

"What I don't understand is how a woman like Lady Ridgeway, so well educated and so in love with books and ideas herself, as her letters to me indisputably show, could allow her daughter to be raised in such ignorance. It just doesn't seem right, does it? One thing to let her own poetic nature be suppressed. But quite another, and very cowardly too, to allow her daughter to be raised as ignorant as a Hottentot."

Gwynneth was speechless for a moment, and could only mirror his dark, troubled stare. How, indeed? Finally she managed to choke out, "Perhaps she was afraid of her husband."

"That is the obvious answer. Yet she dared somehow to read widely and deeply herself, and continues to do so. I managed a peak at their library the night of the ball. It is quite well stocked."

"Yes, she's been an excellent customer," Gwynneth murmured.

"And she must manage to get around that cretin of a husband of hers somehow, to buy and read the books herself!"

"Well, I think Lady Ridgeway can fairly well do as she pleases, as long as she doesn't interfere with her husband's hunting."

"Precisely!" Langley jumped on the point with a thump of his hand on the table. "She's not afraid to brave him to entice me to marry Virginia, either, apparently. You can't tell me I'm *his* idea of the perfect son-in-law."

"Perhaps Virginia really hasn't shown much interest in education before?"

"Of course she hasn't. Interest must be nurtured. Children must be encouraged, even forced, into acquiring education, or they'll all grow up like Hottentots, males as well as females. That's why women often have such an inferior understanding. They simply aren't pushed to think in a logical manner. Miss Wollstonecraft was quite right in this matter."

Gwynneth was silent. Her position was false. She couldn't come up with a plausible reason to cover a situation that didn't really exist.

"Confess to me, Miss Dunlevvy. Don't you find yourself a bit disappointed in our mutual friend for such cowardly neglect?"

Though feeling the greatest hypocrite on earth, Gwynneth took her text straight from one of her father's sermons. "Lord Langley, I believe it is never wise to pass judgment on our fellow creatures. We simply cannot know all their circumstances or feel all the conflicting claims and pressures that pull at them."

Langley's brow cleared. He looked at her with such appreciation, such gratitude, that once more her conscience scorched her. "You are very right, Miss Dunlevvy. 'Judge not,' as the Bible says. You are a clergyman's daughter, and perhaps even that rare person who tries to live the gospel rather than merely quote it."

Gwynneth ducked her head, made even more miserable by this undeserved praise. But Lord Langley leaned across the narrow space that separated them and lifted her chin with one finger. "How fortunate Lady Ridgeway and I are to both have you for a confidante. Perhaps you would ask her . . ."

"No, no." Gwynneth shook her head emphatically. "I did not seek this role, and I certainly won't become a go-between. For one thing, Lady Ridgeway wouldn't permit it."

"No, I don't suppose she will. When I get back to London, I will write and ask her about it."

"Speaking of writing, I wrote Carter Grantham, a noted defender of the press, asking him to join us here at his earliest convenience. I expect he will arrive in a couple of days. I will ask him to assist you in responding to Sir Miles's charges."

"Thank you, Lord Langley. Sir Miles Barlow makes my blood run cold. He threatened to involve Mr. Highley, too, just because he refused to let the man drag me into a private conference."

Langley's lips thinned with anger. "When did this occur?"

"At the same time as he made the threats I told you about in my note. He implied that I could . . . could head off any accusations if I would just . . . just . . ." Gwynneth was too embarrassed to go on, and looked away, tears in her eyes.

"That devil." Langley sat forward, elbows on his knees, and took her hands in his. "Don't worry, my dear. Carter Grantham will know how to deal with his accusations. And I will deal with his improper advances, and so you must tell him if he insults you again."

"Thank you." Gwynneth could hardly speak for the lump in her throat. Sometimes he really seemed kind. Which was he, the man who offered now to protect her from insult, or the one who had himself threatened to kiss her on a public street only minutes before Barlow's insult?

Langley stood, again thanking her for her willingness to listen, and then almost as an afterthought asked her to ride with him the next morning.

"One of the horses I brought with me is a fine little mare, just right for a lady's mount. I brought her for . . . That is, I had hoped that Miss Allen . . ." He broke off in confusion. "No matter. Put on your habit and be ready to go at ten o'clock."

"I couldn't," Gwynneth refused, though she felt a surge of eager desire to accept.

"Nonsense, why not?"

"Propriety again, sir. Unfortunately, I must be a model of respectability to keep the custom of the gentry and burghers of this narrow little town."

"No impropriety will be committed. You are to join Lady Ridgeway, Miss Ridgeway, and several of Mr. Verleigh's guests as well."

Gwynneth gave a start. "Oh, mercy, I couldn't."

"Why not? They will accept you. In fact, I told Lady Ridgeway I might invite you, and she said it was a good idea."

Gwynneth was perplexed at this, but still shook her head. "The others will cut me. It would be too painful."

"I am sure you are mistaken, but if so, then we will cut them in return. Why deny yourself a treat because others are foolish?"

He was a very persuasive man. By now he had returned to stand in front of her, and his deep voice was warm and cajoling. He took her hand. "You are a lady born, Miss Dunlevvy. Hold up your head. If others snub you, it is very much their loss."

"No." Gwynneth shook her head angrily. "Please do not distress me with further pleading. I learned quite abruptly and painfully the chasm that had opened between me and polite society when I became a bookseller's daughter. I don't even *want* to try to bridge the gap. I would far rather keep my place than have someone else put me in it."

"I'm truly sorry. Perhaps I've pressed you too hard." He patted her hand in an avuncular fashion that nevertheless had a most unsettling effect on her breathing. "Well, then, ride with me tomorrow afternoon. I'll bring a groom. We'll be properly chaperoned. Now I won't take no to this," he ended firmly.

She met his eyes and once more felt herself drowning in those chocolate depths. She found herself agreeing without quite being aware of it, and was rewarded with a blinding smile before he bowed to her and took his leave.

Gwynneth's sense of loss of control of the situation escalated later that day when an urgent summon came from Lady Ridgeway, delivered by a footman with orders to take her back in her ladyship's carriage immediately if at all possible.

Chapter Fourteen

Gwynneth would have liked to ignore Lady Ridgeway's summons, but she was well and truly caught now in the strange game of deception she had unwittingly started. She would have to know what Lady Ridgeway wanted, what she planned.

When Gwynneth was escorted into a small, modishly furnished sitting room, Lady Ridgeway characteristically lost no time in getting to the point. "Lord Langley took the bait, Miss Dunlevvy, but now Virginia needs help in setting the hook."

Gwynneth winced at this piscine imagery, but kept quiet, listening as Lady Ridgeway explained, with much excited interrupting by Virginia, the results of their first assault on Lord Langley.

"And so he suggested a list of books she should read, even wrote them out, though he said I should be able to select them for her. Well, Miss Dunlevvy, I thought you were keeping me current with all the new books, but I don't recognize any of these but Shakespeare." Lady Ridgeway sounded indignant and betrayed.

Gwynneth scanned the list her hostess proffered her, with great difficulty suppressing a smile as she did so, for in Lord Langley's bold handwriting she saw a list of the classics of Greek and Roman literature.

"Timeless choices, Lady Ridgeway. He's given her a foundation list, a sort of basic elementary primer for the ed-

ucated person. I assume he means her to read these in translation. You don't read Latin or Greek, Virginia?"

"No, indeed, and do you know Lord Langley looked
quite surprised and disappointed that I don't. He suggested
I get a tutor and begin learning them, Latin at least. As if I
want to go back to the schoolroom now!" Virginia's lower
lip protruded sulkily.

"Can you get these books for us, Miss Dunlevvy." Lady
Ridgeway cut across her daughter's whine impatiently.

"I shouldn't be surprised if you don't have most of them
already. But it will take months for Virginia to read and
comprehend all of this."

"Months! I don't have months," stormed Virginia.

Simultaneously her mother boomed, "Exactly so. Which
is why we'll need your help, Miss Dunlevvy."

"My help," Gwynneth squeaked. "How can I . . . ?" She
knew the answer but sought time while she looked for a
way out of this uncomfortable situation.

"You've read these books?"

"Yes, of course. That is, they are standard . . ."

Unaware that Gwynneth's hesitation was an effort to
avoid hurting her feelings by exposing the deficiency in her
education, Lady Ridgeway plowed straight ahead. "Then
you'll summarize them for her as you do for me when you
deliver new books."

"I'm to ride with him tomorrow," Virginia added. "I
must have something to say to him."

"He'll never believe you've read all those books or even
one of them in so little time. The *Iliad* and the *Odyssey,*
which he has suggested you begin with, are both quite
long."

"I can at least show him I've begun." Virginia's persis-
tence showed that she was, despite a young girl's shyness,
her mother's daughter.

"Yes, Miss Dunlevvy. Summarize one of them for her,
right now."

In the end, Gwynneth summarized the *Iliad* for Virginia, insisting she read as much of it for herself as she could before the morrow. They went into the library, which as Lord Langley had observed, was well stocked, for each generation of Ridgeways, however little inclined to be bookish, seemed to have been determined their library make a decent showing.

Gwynneth helped Virginia locate Chapman's translation of Homer. "The thing to do, Virginia, instead of trying to appear that you have absorbed so massive a work so quickly, is to ask him some questions. He'll be very happy, I am sure, to explain it to you. I'll give you some interesting textual questions."

Lady Ridgeway agreed enthusiastically. "That is the plan. Get him interested in you by showing your eagerness to learn."

Virginia sighed. "What will I do once we're married? I can't be always running to Miss Dunlevvy for help."

"Once he's properly leg-shackled, it won't matter," Lady Ridgeway snapped.

Gwynneth felt a shudder run through her. She believed and hoped Lord Langley was in no danger from these machinations. She would feel really terrible if he were to get such a wife by her interference.

After she had written out a few questions to help Virginia read the *Iliad* and discuss it intelligently, she returned to her shop hoping against hope that Lord Langley would go to London immediately so she could return to a normal, honest existence.

When Lord Langley and the other members of Mr. Verleigh's party met Lady Ridgeway and Virginia for their ride, Virginia was quick to engage her quarry in a discussion of the *Iliad*. Pleased by her interest, Lord Langley began to expound on the first of her questions, regarding Achilles. Was he behaving like a spoiled child to withhold himself from battle, or was he justified by the blow his pride had received at the distribution of prizes? The question of honor versus duty clearly fascinated Lord Langley.

But riding horseback with a lively group of people, many of whom were of decidedly unintellectual bent, makes serious discussion impossible, and Langley soon found himself suggesting that he call on Virginia for the purpose of continuing their talk. She immediately asked him to accompany them home for nuncheon.

Lady Ridgeway was extremely pleased with her daughter's progress with Lord Langley. She beamed on them both benevolently, easily dodged his lordship's suggestion that she take part in the discussion after their meal, and left them private in the library, the door ajar for form's sake.

Virginia had studied Gwynneth's list of questions carefully and had read some of the *Iliad* herself. All she had to do was ask her handsome guest questions and listen to his answers with a suitably enthralled look on her face. Virginia did not find this difficult, as just looking at his appealingly masculine features enthralled her.

Langley was disappointed but not surprised that Lady Ridgeway did not join them for their discussion. She had never once wavered from her intention of treating him as a new acquaintance, but she clearly wanted him for a son-in-law. The baron wasn't interested in Virginia, but he felt an obligation to help the poor child out of the abyss of ignorance her mother had so unconscionably allowed her to fall into.

He was pleasantly surprised by the girl's progress, too. Her insightful questions showed a mind capable of getting to the essence of things. As he talked enthusiastically, a gesticulation caught Virginia's copy of the *Iliad* on the corner and flipped it off the table.

When it fell, a sheet of paper that had been folded in it slipped out and floated across the floor. He retrieved it, noting that it had writing on both sides.

He started to hand it to his pupil when the handwriting caught his eye. Abruptly he stopped and looked sharply at Virginia. "What is this?"

Virginia flushed and bit her lip. "Those are my questions. You see, I . . . well, I made notes as I read along." He scowled at her and she hurried on, "to help me think about it and to ask you if I couldn't figure out . . . that is . . ." Her voice trailed off as he looked at her sternly.

"Now, Virginia, I know this isn't your handwriting. I recognize it very well. There is nothing wrong with her helping you in your studies, though why she hasn't done so before now, I can't imagine, but I am disappointed in your lack of honesty. Could it possibly be that you have been doing a bit of scheming?"

Virginia was deeply embarrassed, mortified, in fact. "Please don't be angry, Lord Langley. I only wanted to make a good impression, and mother knew how clever Miss Dunlevvy is, so she asked her to help me."

"What has Miss Dunlevvy to do with this?"

"She . . . you said you recognized her handwriting."

"If you are trying to protect your mother, you may as well know I have already guessed her identity. I confess I am amazed she let you in on it, though. That's placing a great deal of reliance on a young girl's discretion."

"What? I don't know what you are talking about."

"And if she could trust you with our secret, obviously she could have trusted you to learn the classics without your father's knowing. Why are you not better educated? Did you have no wish to learn, even with your mother's magnificent education as an example?"

Virginia began to suspect Lord Langley was slightly mad. "Secret? You have some sort of secret with my mother? Is Miss Dunlevvy involved in it, too?"

"That's the second time you've mentioned Miss Dunlevvy. What has she to do with any of this?" Langley ran his hand through his hair in frustration.

"It was when you recognized her handwriting that you began to . . . to . . . scold and . . ." Virginia was near tears.

"I recognized your mother's handwriting." He slapped the piece of paper for emphasis. "Don't think to fob me off!"

"No! Miss Dunlevvy wrote these questions for me. Mother asked her to help because . . ."

Lady Ridgeway may have been as scheming a matchmaker as Lord Langley had ever encountered, but she was by no means a careless mother. She was not far from the door and by this time had heard the angry sounds coming from the library. She hurried in. "What is going on?"

"Tell me, madam. Who wrote this?" Langley was standing now, his look burningly intense.

Lady Ridgeway looked down at the questions he brandished and then into Lord Langley's agitated countenance.

"Clumsy girl," she turned on Virginia. "Why on earth did you let him see those."

"The point is, I have seen them. Now without further roundaboutation, who wrote them."

"Lord Langley, don't enact a Cheltenham tragedy. Virginia wished to know you better, that is all. It was Miss Dunlevvy who suggested that . . ."

"Then you are saying Miss Dunlevvy wrote this paper?"

"Yes, but you refine on it too much entirely."

"Oh, no, Lady Ridgeway. I don't refine on it nearly enough. I will have the truth if I have to show this document to your husband and ask *him* for the author."

"And how, pray tell, is my husband to know Miss Dunlevvy's handwriting?" Lady Ridgeway's resentment of her guest's manner began to show in her voice.

The truth was beginning to be very clear to Langley. Drawing a deep breath for patience, he asked in a less threatening tone, "The invitation you sent Nicholas for your ball. Did Miss Dunlevvy also write that?"

"For heaven's sake, such a fuss. Yes, the gel often acts as an amanuensis for me. My own writing is dreadful if you must know. But pray tell me why do you place so much significance on this?"

"Lady Ridgeway, I ask you now for the truth. Have you, either with or without the help of an amanuensis, been corresponding with me?"

"I?" Lady Ridgeway's face became brick red. "Corresponding with you? About what, pray tell? Only just met you."

"You've never sent me poetry for publication in *The Legacy*?"

The matron sputtered her utter incredulity as her daughter giggled. "P-p-poetry? Me? Young man, you have windmills in your head."

Lord Langley felt a strong sense of relief wash over him as he realized she was telling him the truth. Lady Ridgeway had never fit his idea of what "Miss Allen" should be. Substituting Miss Dunlevvy's age and personality made a much more believable fit. The urge to jump up and give a triumphant shout was difficult to suppress.

But now he had to get out of an embarrassing situation. Carefully schooling his features into polite contrition, he apologized to the matron and her daughter. "Of course. I beg your pardon. You see, this paper was written by a hand very similar to that of a young woman who wrote to my magazine, enclosing some charming poems, anonymously."

"Miss Dunlevvy," Virginia breathed, relieved to have the mystery solved.

"Wouldn't doubt it for a minute," Lady Ridgeway agreed. "Gel is frightfully bookish."

Lord Langley subsided into the chair next to Virginia. "Since she wants the poems to be anonymous, suppose we three never let on. I own I'm glad to know who wrote them, because they are exquisite, but I wouldn't want to cause her any embarrassment. Particularly as she was so kind as to help Virginia with her studies." He smiled at the two with all the considerable charm at his command and picked up the book again.

Mother and daughter were relieved to see him returning to the role of Virginia's mentor, though both were rather wary after this display of volatility. They appeared perfectly content to leave Miss Dunlevvy and her poetry in obscurity.

When he was alone at last, cantering back to the Verleigh estate, Lord Langley allowed his anger at being tricked by Miss Dunlevvy full rein. His indignation boiled. How dare she pretend Lady Ridgeway had written those exquisite lines. Had she laughed at him for believing it of that improbable, ignorant, horsey matron? What a dance she had led him! His mind roamed back over their various conversations, examining the various double entendres, half-truths, and outright lies Miss Dunlevvy had employed to deceive him. All a May Game!

He felt he had been made a fool of, and that led to a thirst for revenge. Not that he was sorry to learn that Gwynneth Dunlevvy was his Miss Allen. Oh, no! In fact, he was quite pleased about it. All sorts of interesting possibilities occurred to him as a result of that knowledge. Perhaps he should just go to her, confront her with his knowledge, and scold her thoroughly.

Langley contemplated this scene and its possible finale with pleasure for a few minutes, but then his lips curled derisively. Doubtless the little witch would still find some way to fob him off, to deny the truth. He must think carefully of a plan, a way to get back a little of his own for the grief she had given him, and at the same time smoke her out into the open once and for all.

Chapter Fifteen

Gwynneth prepared for her ride with Lord Langley with a mixture of eagerness and trepidation. He had only befriended her because of what he believed of her relationship to Lady Ridgeway. What would be his attitude toward her if he knew the truth? Would he renew his attempts to seduce her, or would he be too furious at the deception? Neither outcome was desirable. The man's pride would probably never let him forgive her for the hoax. And if he would be an invaluable ally as a friend, he would doubtless be a most unpleasant enemy.

Yet she wanted desperately to go. She told herself it was only because she wanted the pleasure of riding a fine horse again. The pleasure of his lordship's company was entirely beside the point.

She allowed Lord Langley to toss her into the saddle, feeling a little frisson of excitement run through her at his strong hands around her waist. She self-consciously busied herself arranging the skirts of her habit while her heart rate returned to normal. As they began to move through the streets of Guilford, his groom trailing well behind, she patted the neck of the fine, dainty mare she was riding.

"She's a sweetheart. What is her name?"

"Pinky, believe it or not." Langley's eyebrows arched and his mouth curved in a mischievous smile.

"Pinky! You're bamming me." She patted the sleek dappled gray neck.

"When she was newborn, she was so nearly white her skin shone through and made her look pink. Even today when she is wet, she takes on a pinkish-gray cast. So the name stuck."

Laughing, Gwynneth forgot to be shy or worried. "And that handsome fellow you are riding. Is he called Red?"

Langley grinned. "No, he answers to Turk."

As they cleared the town and she felt the breeze on her cheeks, Gwynneth forgot everything but the pleasures of riding a fine horse. Langley, in turn, gave himself up to the pleasure of watching this comely young woman, suddenly metamorphized into his "Miss Allen." She looked a treat on horseback. That green habit outlining her figure in ways that almost drove all thought of revenge from his head, the joy in those golden eyes, the nimbus of nearly white-blond hair that had escaped confinement to encircle her head like a crown, all delighted him.

Langley steered her onto Nicholas's land. "Do you hunt, Miss Dunlevvy?"

"I love the chase, though I have no enthusiasm for the kill."

Langley nodded approvingly. "I abhor blood sports myself. I sometimes ride along to please my host, however. Like you, I love a good run. In fact, let us race to the clump of trees beyond the third wall."

Gwynneth took up his challenge instantly. How she loved the feeling of floating, of flying, as she and Pinky took the three hurdles. Langley caught up with her but made no real effort to pass her until they were within yards of the trees, when a sudden burst of speed put his long-legged gelding ahead.

Breathless, laughing, they turned by common consent and walked their horses companionably. "You have a fine seat," Langley said.

"Thank you. I feel I am in heaven. It has been so long." Her eyes sparkled with pleasure.

"Lady Ridgeway is a fine horsewoman, too." He watched her carefully, catching the little flicker of a shadow across her face.

"Yes, I believe she is."

"I am looking forward to watching her ride to the hounds next week."

"I am sure you are." Gwynneth glanced away, biting her lips. "How did your discussion with Virginia go this morning?"

"Ah, you knew about that? It went well. In fact, I joined them for nuncheon, and we spent quite an hour afterward discussing the *Iliad*. Virginia is a brighter girl than first appears. Such intelligent questions as she had. Like mother, like daughter, I suppose. With a husband like me to encourage her instead of oppress her, she might even exceed Lady Ridgeway, who knows? I confess, it makes me feel the need to reexamine some of my views. If marriage can be slavery for some, perhaps it can be liberation for others."

Langley hoped his auditor would feel sufficient shame at promoting a false match to confess her identity. More than anything he yearned to acknowledge Gwynneth as his "Miss Allen" so they could have the first of many fascinating conversations. But she must be the one to confess the truth.

Astonished to hear him hint at marriage to Miss Ridgeway, Gwynneth turned her head slightly to prevent Lord Langley from seeing her dismay. If he fell for Virginia, supposing her to be what she most definitely was not, how would Gwynneth bear the guilt of her role in such a misalliance?

"In fact, I have worked it out. I believe that is what Lady Ridgeway hopes for in seeking to attach me to the child—a husband who will encourage her daughter to become a rational, educated human being. I must admit, the idea begins to tempt me." Surely now she would speak. She couldn't possibly countenance his being caught in such a dishonorable way, in such an uneven match.

"Perhaps." Gwynneth drew in a deep, shuddering breath and looked away, biting her lower lip. Her mind was racing, looking for a solution, but she saw none. She did not know what he might do if she confessed her identity: seduce her, physically chastise her, abandon her to Sir Miles Barlow? Yet she couldn't abandon him to Virginia Ridgeway, either. Pulled strongly in opposite directions, Gwynneth could not act. A silence fell between them.

She isn't going to say anything. She'd let me fall for that featherbrain, marry her, and be damned. Renewed fury surged through Lord Langley and all his vengeful feelings returned. He fought hard to gain control of his tone of voice as he set his plan of revenge in motion.

"Nicholas is planning an early hunt to entertain his guests. Why do you not join us? You can ride Pinky."

Gwynneth was glad of the change of subjects, but determined to refuse. "I have already told you, Lord Langley, I am not eager to receive snubs."

"But Nicholas told me anyone who can sit a horse is welcome at his hunt. Besides, you shouldn't let the fear of snubs prevent you from the friendships that would also be offered. It is not very brave of you, Miss Dunlevvy."

She looked into his suddenly stern face. "I am not very brave, Lord Langley."

"No, you are not." His voice was harsh. In fact, he looked furious at having his invitation rejected.

"I have my reasons, my lord!" She gave Pinky a light tap with her heels, and the mare cantered past the groom, who was just now catching up with them. Gwynneth set her course for home, and Lord Langley followed. When he pulled abreast of her, he reached out a hand, gesturing for her to stop.

"A moment, Miss Dunlevvy."

She turned, her small chin thrust out at him defiantly, but drew her horse up.

"Forgive me. I did not mean to distress you. I am just feeling very out of patience with feminine timidity right now."

"How so, my lord?"

"Oh, Lady Ridgeway's refusal to acknowledge me as her friend is costing us both some precious time together. Soon I must return to London, and we may never meet again. It's so damnably frustrating!"

Relief flooded her. This did not sound like he expected to become a part of Lady Ridgeway's family by marriage. "But she said she would write you again once you left the area."

"Yes. Though it will hardly supplant the pleasure to be had from untrammeled conversation, I suppose that must content me."

They rode in silence for quite a while, each deep in troubled thought. When they turned onto Gwynneth's street, she began to thank him.

"No, don't. I wish I could arrange for you to ride often. We must do so again before I leave the area. It is a small thank you, for without your assistance and discretion, I might not be able to continue my correspondence with Lady Ridgeway."

She forced herself to look into his eyes. "Is it so important to you, then?"

"Indeed it is. I don't know how to explain it, but something in her mind completes something in mine. We call to each other like two halves of a whole."

Gwynneth was deeply affected by this comment, which unknown to her handsome companion was about herself, not Lady Ridgeway. It expressed something she had often felt when reading his letters to her. Perhaps she was being unnecessarily timid and distrustful. Could anyone who felt thus be a brutal, ruthless seducer? He had offered her friendship often; could it be that he would keep to just that, if she asked him?

She was drawing breath to speak, to confess all, when he continued in a musing tone, "I never much believed in platonic friendships, but now I find myself involved in one, and it both perplexes and frustrates me." Lord Langley shook his head. "I am uncertain how to proceed; I suppose I must simply resume the correspondence and let it rest at that, since she seems entirely uninterested in a more intimate connection. She is committed to her marriage, her children, her life here. I must respect that."

Any temptation to confess her identity to him was quickly quashed by this remark. If he accepted a platonic friendship so reluctantly from Lady Ridgeway, she knew instinctively he would not do so at all with herself.

He dismounted and helped her down. As she stood on her threshold, he took her hand. "Promise me something, Miss Dunlevvy."

"If I can, Lord Langley."

"If Lady Ridgeway is ever in trouble, ever has a problem with her husband that I might solve—by eloping with her or putting a bullet through him if necessary—please let me know."

Gwynneth shuddered, looking into the now hard, determined eyes. "I am mortally certain she will never want that, sir."

"But promise me—if she is in real distress—I would not hesitate to risk all to assist her. You must promise."

Gwynneth was both touched and alarmed by this protestation. He looked entirely capable of such drastic measures. "I . . . I promise, Lord Langley."

He drew her hand to his lips for a quick, fervent kiss. "Thank you, Miss Dunlevvy. Once again you prove a true friend."

Once again, thought Gwynneth, I've proved myself a

true liar and traitor. Thank God, he'd be gone soon, out of Lady Ridgeway's sphere and her own.

Langley rode back to Nicholas's smiling to himself. He had set the stage very nicely. Miss Dunlevvy had a great surprise and a great shock coming to her next week. He would shake the truth out of that devious, lying little minx and then . . . yes, revenge would be very sweet.

Mr. Carter Grantham looked appreciatively around the vast entryway of Nicholas Verleigh's mansion. There was a great deal to be said for new money! So much marble, so much ormolu, and all so new and modern in design. It seemed that Nicholas's father had not only been a man of great acumen when it came to the buying and selling of land, but a man with a free hand when it came to the spending of the money he had gained thereby.

Mr. Grantham was from a very old family, but had inherited nothing but fine bloodlines and a keen intellect, so he had gone into the law. Whiggish tendencies and excellent connections had allied themselves to necessity to make him the man to whom liberal aristocrats like Lord Langley turned for legal advice.

Grantham mopped his red face. It was hot, and he was very heavy, which made the heat all the more unbearable. "Carter, so glad you could come promptly." Langley moved toward him looking annoyingly cool and graceful, but Grantham accepted the outstretched hand gladly.

"Devilish time to pick to ask me to leave London. What a time we are having there, with crowned heads of state and military heroes as thick as fleas. Grand celebrations of some sort every night."

"Which is precisely why I am here!"

"But the spectacle! Stuart, you should see the mob clamoring for old Blucher. Man cannot go anywhere but they must unhitch his horses and draw his carriage through the street."

"I am indeed sorry to tear you away from such an edify-ing sight." Langley's mouth quirked in a way that indicated little sympathy with his portly friend and adviser.

He led Grantham into a small drawing room and ordered a cooling glass of lemonade to be brought. "Matter is ur-gent, Carter. As I told you in my letter, the government, in the person of Sir Miles Barlow, is about to make a martyr of a young lady who is without friend or fortune, in their excess zeal to control the press."

"So you said. I've heard they are drafting even more se-vere laws, plus planning to double the tax on newspapers."

"They'll be completely out of the reach of most people then. I take it that is the idea."

"Precisely. And you say Barlow is involved. That's un-fortunate. He is as zealous as a Spanish inquisitor, I fear."

The two discussed the situation at length. As they talked, Nicholas, John, and Roger joined them, each roundly con-demning the government and its agent, Barlow.

"You realize, gentlemen, that Barlow hopes to implicate all of you in the matter, if Stuart reads his insinuations cor-rectly? The fact that Nicholas has admittedly written for the paper when Dunlevvy was alive makes the matter even more dangerous. Might be best not to become involved in this young woman's fight." Grantham knew he was whistling in the wind, but felt it was his duty to warn these young enthusiasts.

He mopped his brow. It was still hot in spite of the cool-ing lemonade and the wide-open windows. "I was able to obtain some copies of the scurrilous rag in London. Thing is, gentlemen, this particular publication is so vile that you will not find any sympathy from any English jury that can be convinced you had a hand in its printing."

"Can't make up a case out of whole cloth," Roger in-sisted.

"No, but the case against the girl has some plausibility, I believe."

"Indeed it does. Unless you take the young woman's character into account." Langley was surer than ever of Miss Dunlevvy's innocence now that he knew her to be "Miss Allen."

"If they can succeed in making a good case against her, and the four of you rush to her defense, they might well pull you down with her."

Roger looked decidedly alarmed at this, but Nicholas began to chuckle. "What rot! Might get me, a commoner after all, but two peers of the realm, convicted and imprisoned on the same grounds as a mere bookseller, without the most ironclad of proofs! You are letting what ought to be blind you to what is!"

Langley nodded his agreement. "Sir Miles will catch cold at that game, it is true, but Miss Dunlevvy could suffer the worse because he is frustrated in his more ambitious prey."

Grantham shot a shrewd look at Langley. "Pretty, is she?"

Langley made an annoyed gesture. "An attractive female. No diamond, but of more than passing interest. But she could have two heads, and Miles would want her if he thought it would upset me. He's set himself up as my rival since grammar school."

"And lost every time, lad," John growled.

"Well, I must meet this female and decide for myself if she is defensible. For the publication, I assure you, is not. And I'll not put my good name on the line for a woman with more charm than scruples."

"Once you've met her you'll have no more doubts, Carter. She's a very prim-and-proper lady." Langley smiled confidently at the lawyer.

"I'll order the carriage brought around." Nicholas sprang to his feet.

"Steady, Nick. Carter is looking quite done in, and it's late." Langley indicated the clock ticking on the mantel. "Let him recoup himself, and we'll go over tomorrow. I'll send Miss Dunlevvy a note to expect us."

Chapter Sixteen

What Gwynneth hoped for when she eagerly tore open the note in Langley's bold scrawl, she wasn't sure. But her eagerness quickly faded when she comprehended the formally worded request to call on her with his respected legal adviser, Carter Grantham, Sunday afternoon.

Somehow she dreaded this interview. It would give substance to what she had thus far chosen to see as Sir Miles Barlow's rather insane imaginings. But she was appreciative of Langley's support, and quickly penned a note welcoming their visit.

When the group of men entered her office, she faced them somewhat nervously. She had dressed in the newest result of her sewing efforts, a very modest dove-gray morning dress, and wore a demure cap on her carefully braided flaxen hair.

"Won't you come upstairs, gentlemen. We can be more comfortable in my parlor, I believe."

When all were seated, Grantham began to quiz her on the matter of the posthumous *Register*. Preventing Langley from joining in with a firm shake of his head, he drew from Gwynneth all that she knew. He was particularly insistent in asking if she had written anything, anything at all, for the newspaper.

Cheeks pink, eyes averted, Gwynneth shook her head. How she wished Lord Langley weren't here. She could tell Grantham about her market day essay, which she supposed had been among her father's papers at the office when he became ill. She had given it to him to read over before submitting it to *The Legacy*.

But with Langley looking on, she could not tell the lawyer this, or her secret would be out, for the perceptive baron had instantly recognized her style in the essay.

"I have given some thought to the matter, Mr. Grantham, and have decided that the Irish pressman that my father employed must have something to do with these forged issues of the *Register*. Sir Miles told me that he had arrested the man. I believe he may have implicated me. He was quite furious with me for discontinuing the paper, and not just because it meant the loss of his livelihood. There is something of the zealot in the man."

Grantham nodded. "That could well be, Miss Dunlevvy." He was making notes in a small notebook as they talked; he carefully wrote down the man's name.

"But do you have any idea, Miss Dunlevvy, how they could have operated the press without anyone knowing it? In a small town such as this, surely such a thing must have been remarked."

"I heard no mention of it. You assume it is my father's press that was used, but . . ."

"I've done some comparing on my own, Miss Dunlevvy, using past issues of the *Register* in Mr. Verleigh's library and some copies of the posthumous ones that I purchased in London. I strongly feel that the two were printed on the same press. Let me show you."

Grantham struggled to raise his bulky body from the chair and took several papers from a large portfolio he had brought. Laying them out on Gwynneth's desk, he pointed out letters that had the exact same irregularities in the two different issues.

Gwynneth could hardly bring herself to look at his evidence, for it required looking at the blatantly vulgar articles that described in vivid details the supposed amours of the

Prince Regent and various members of the cabinet. Turning away quickly, she murmured, "I shall take your word for it, sir."

The others crowded around, and were quickly convinced of the truth of Grantham's analysis. Dudley whistled apprehensively. "I say, that looks bad, don't it, Stu?"

"How can this have been done without anyone being aware of it?" There was a note in McDougal's voice that clearly indicated doubt of Gwynneth's innocence.

Lord Langley turned toward the alarmed girl. "I have an idea. Don't look so frightened, Miss Dunlevvy. I believe in you implicitly."

Gwynneth let those chocolate eyes warm and steady her. "Thank you, sir. But I can understand your suspicions, gentlemen. It all seems rather incriminating."

"What is your idea, Stuart?" Grantham gathered the papers and replaced all but one in his portfolio.

"I remember when we entered the press that there were very heavy black draperies above the windows. I thought it odd, as one would have expected the press to need all of the daylight that could be shed on the room. The significance didn't really dawn on me at that time. No one has seen the press in operation because it has been run at dead of night, with those draperies drawn."

Deep masculine voices rumbled as this idea was discussed. Gwynneth sat back in her chair, relieved. "That must be it!"

"Possibly." Grantham's voice and expression still indicated skepticism. "But Miss Dunlevvy, I must ask you again, did you write anything that appeared in this paper."

"Give over, Carter. You saw that she could barely look at the trash." Nicholas's feelings of chivalry were aroused.

Gwynneth's denial was on her lips, but as she looked into the heavyset lawyer's flushed face, she could see that he would not believe her. She hesitated, on the verge of revealing all to him.

Before she could quite nerve herself to do so, Langley intervened. "Yes, let it go. We've been over this ground several times. Miss Dunlevvy is not a writer, at any rate. All she ever did for the newspaper was keep the accounts, is that not correct?"

"I . . . yes, yes, that is correct." She swung her eyes to meet Langley's, and was startled to see that they were twinkling with some inexplicable amusement.

"Well, I think we have done what we can here. I shall try to speak to Sir Miles. Perhaps he will reveal his hand to me. Mr. Verleigh, you are the magistrate here. Has this Irishman been charged?"

"No, but under this rotten system he does not have to be charged with a crime to be jailed. Sir Miles has the authority to jail him without charges and without bail, merely on suspicion."

Angry growls accompanied this, as the four men trailed Grantham out of Gwynneth's office and into the bookstore. At the door to the shop, Langley turned and chucked Gwynneth under the chin. "Buck up, Miss Dunlevvy. Grantham is the best, and we are not without influence."

"I thank you, sir, for taking my part."

Oh, my. Those eyes, Langley thought. Just now they were huge and, in the light pouring through the window, all the shades of blue, green, brown, and gold that make up that ambiguous designation "hazel" could be seen in them. With difficulty he resisted pulling the unhappy chit into his arms. Surprised at the depths of his feelings, and even more surprised that they were as protective as they were amorous, he turned abruptly and followed his friends into the street.

As Nicholas's overly full carriage bore the five men back to his home, Langley noted that the lawyer was quiet, his round moon of a face unusually solemn. "Out with it, Carter. What's bothering you?"

"She's lying."

"What?" "No!" The other voiced indignation, but Langley waited, every nerve on edge. When it became clear the lawyer would not continue, he asked impatiently, "What makes you think so."

"I can see it. Plain as a pikestaff, on her face. Guilt written all over her."

Lord Langley dropped back against the squabs of the carriage, dejected. Carter Grantham was as shrewd a judge of human nature as he had ever met, and he had made the judgment of character from facial expressions and body posture a particular study. "I've rarely known you to be wrong, Carter," he began.

"And I'm not wrong now. She's not telling the truth, and I'm not taking a case that has me defending anyone involved in a filthy bit of trash like this. You are taken with the chit, I can see that well enough, but that has nothing to say to her innocence."

Pain lanced through Langley at the thought of his cherished correspondent being involved in such a scurrilous enterprise. It couldn't be! It was entirely out of character, wasn't it? And yet . . . she had certainly behaved in a deceptive manner ever since he came to Guilford, letting him chase Lady Ridgeway down a long blind alley of falsehood.

Deeply disillusioned, he stared out the window. The carriage ride ended in silence, and Verleigh stood by Langley watching while Grantham ponderously climbed the stairs to rest awhile before luncheon. "Could I have a word, Stu?"

Seeing that he wished to be private, the other two men took themselves off to find the ladies. A solemn Stuart watched Nicholas pour them both a brandy and then pace with his in his hand.

"Well, Nick. Cut line. Obviously something is on your mind."

"I think I know why Miss Dunlevvy couldn't look Carter in the face when asked whether she had written any of that newspaper."

Langley watched his friend without comment, knowing that he was enjoying this moment. Nothing pleased him more than solving a puzzle that was eluding someone else. It would be useless to try to hurry him, impatient as he was to hear the explanation.

"Did you not tell me that you thought Lady Ridgeway had written a piece that had somehow found its way into the paper? A young woman with an active conscience might feel she should reveal that bit of information, yet with her loyalty to Lady Ridgeway, she couldn't."

Of Course! Relief poured into Langley as he realized why Miss Dunlevvy had looked guilty to Carter. But he had not told Nicholas yet of his discovery that "Miss Allen" was not Lady Ridgeway. Would his friend be able to guess that she was Gwynneth? He had been planning on taking Nick into his confidence in order to obtain his help in setting up his revenge on Miss Dunlevvy. Now he was curious to see where Nick's powers of deduction would lead him.

"Yes, Nick, but if you recall, she vehemently denied it in her letter to me."

"Well, of course she did. Stands to reason."

"Why is that?"

"Now you are being a chucklehead, Stu. Plain to see that a woman capable of playing such a double game with you could be up to all kinds of mischief and no one would ever believe it of her."

A cold chill passed over Langley. The same could be said of Miss Dunlevvy, couldn't it? But, no. She wasn't the calm cool dissembler that he and Nick had believed Regina Ridgeway to be. In fact, it was her very honesty that had betrayed her into embarrassment when Grantham questioned her.

Once more secure in the knowledge that "Miss Allen" was innocent, he took up Nicholas's line of reasoning. "Let me get this straight." Langley was rather enjoying seeing his friend led down the garden path. "You think Lady

Ridgeway is involved in the publication of the posthumous *Register?*"

"Stands to reason. She's a writer, she has money to put into the venture, and you've already said she's a cool conspirator."

"But what has that to do with Miss Dunlevvy's looking guilty?"

"Honestly, Stu, you are being such a slow-top. You said yourself the gel was touchingly loyal to Regina. Her blushes and confusion were because she didn't want to betray her friend."

Langley chuckled. "It's a pretty good piece of work, Nick. Unfortunately, you're missing a clue or two."

"You just don't like to admit . . ."

"I'll give you another chance at it. Just take my word for this, and I think you can figure it out. Lady Ridgeway did *not* write the essay on market day that was in the scurrilous *Register.*"

"So she told you, but . . ."

"No, you won't get it right until you accept that she did *not* write it."

"But you said yourself they were stylistically similar. Hang it, I know they are. Read it carefully, compared it with that little piece on Bath that she sent you for *The Legacy.*"

"Yes, you are correct."

"So the same person wrote both."

"Yes."

"But Lady Ridgeway didn't?"

"Most definitely not."

Nicholas frowned and paced frenetically. Langley left him to his musings, swirling the brandy in his glass.

"Damn. How long have you known?" Nicholas jumped across the room and confronted his friend in irritation.

"Known what?"

"That Miss Dunlevvy is your poet, damn it."

"Very good, Nick! Very good." He laughed heartily. "I've known since I went home with the ladies Ridgeway for nuncheon Thursday after our ride, remember? Virginia let a slip of paper fall out of her book in the unmistakable handwriting of my 'Miss Allen.' It was a list of questions and comments for her to use when discussing her reading with me.

"When I taxed her about it, she finally admitted she'd had Miss Dunlevvy prepare them to help her attempt to convince me she is a bluestocking." At the absurdity of it all, both men began to laugh. But Langley stopped quickly. "Made a fool of me, Nick. Mean to have a bit of revenge on my pretty bookseller for that."

"I expect her fate at Sir Mile's hands will be revenge enough."

"Whatever can you mean? Don't think I'm annoyed enough to throw her to him, do you?"

"No, but if she wrote that essay . . ."

"Yes?"

"Then she is involved with the illegal newspaper, in spite of her innocent looks." Nicholas's voice was that of a man disgusted with himself for being taken in.

"Nonsense. Mr. Dunlevvy was her father. Perfectly obvious it was something she'd given to him before he died. Probably among his papers at the press. The scoundrel used it for filler in his first issue."

"Of course!" Nick looked vastly relieved. "Didn't want to believe it of Miss Dunlevvy. Especially not if she's the sublimely talented 'Miss Allen.' "

"Here, here!" The two friends toasted one another in perfect charity.

"Wonder why old Martin never recruited her to write for him. 'Fraid I helped the gel deceive you with that bit of false reasoning."

"Perhaps Dunlevvy was prescient enough to avoid exposing his daughter to the danger that she now faces. Ironical, eh?" Langley tossed off the last of his brandy with a wry grin.

"But you'll have to convince Grantham, or he'll not represent her."

Langley frowned. "That may not be as easy as it seems. I'll doubtless have to send for her letters, and get him to read her poetry and essays. Once he knows more about her character, he'll be able to see that she simply couldn't be involved."

"Well, let's go tackle him about it now."

The two friends exited the yellow salon just as a carriage pulled away. Its wheels could be heard spinning in the fine gravel of the carriage-way. A footman approached. "My lord? Mr. Grantham said to give you this."

"Drat!" Langley took the folded, sealed note and ripped it open, perusing it swiftly.

"We can ride after him, Stu."

"No, let him go. He says he doesn't want to be involved, that I've let myself be bewitched by a pretty face, and his reputation won't stand defending such a publication. Rather insulting note, actually, damn his eyes." Langley crushed the letter in his hand. "I doubt he'd change his mind, even if I explained all to him. You know how stubborn Carter can be when he's taken a position."

"Then where are we?"

"We, my friend, are in the suds. But not nearly as badly as our little friend Miss Dunlevvy, I fear."

Chapter Seventeen

Lord Langley knew that he must inform Miss Dunlevvy of Carter Grantham's defection. It was with a pleasant sense of anticipation that he had Pinky saddled early the next morning and ordered a groom to follow him into Guilford. Surely her danger would force her to drop the masquerade, confess that she was his "Miss Allen," and accept the protection he so longed to give her.

A certain uneasiness caused him to shift his big frame uncomfortably in the saddle as he contemplated his plans for her. That pride and strong moral sense that he had found in the letters and observed in the woman, would be seriously challenged by society's reaction to her if he took her as his mistress. Yet he could not drop his lifelong opposition to marriage. He recalled the philosopher Godwin's description of the institution. "It is property, and the worst of property." Never could he forget his father's treatment of his mother. A fine-blooded horse in his stable would have received more consideration. Yet when she had tried to leave him, he had been so infuriated he had banished her to a distant estate, forbidding her to see her children. She had no recourse in law, and had died early, a lonely, bitter woman.

No, he wouldn't cage a woman like that, ever. But he wanted Gwynneth Dunlevvy as he had never wanted another woman. He wanted her body, and he wanted her soul. He would somehow convince her that he was right, that he was looking out for her interests, when he offered her a liaison that was not marriage.

Gwynneth was barely out of bed when she heard a loud banging on the outside rear door. Who could be calling so early on Monday morning? She emerged from her room, tying on a voluminous bright pink robe as Hannah started down the steps, calling over her shoulders, "I'll see to it, miss."

Gwynneth stepped back into her bedroom to bring some order to her tousled hair. She only had time to brush it into a silken smoothness before Hannah was back, a disapproving look on her face. "It's him, Miss Gwynny. That lord."

Behind her Langley towered in the doorway. "Sorry to disturb you so early, Miss Dunlevvy, but I've something very important to tell you."

Flustered by her dishabille, Gwynneth shook her hair back and tied it with a ribbon. "Please await me in the parlor, my lord."

"Very well, but will you put on a riding habit? I've brought Pinky. She's spoiling for a ride. And, of course, I've brought a groom to play propriety."

Gwynneth darted a quick look at his eyes. A moment ago his manner had suggested alarm and concern. Now he seemed lighthearted and almost flirtatious. What a difficult man to read. "Very well, my lord, if you will withdraw." She put on a prim face, and he grinned at her mischievously.

"If you insist, though I'm a dab hand at braids."

Pink-cheeked, Gwynneth shut the door in his face, unaware of just how much Langley ached to touch her silk-textured flaxen hair.

The beldam Hannah harrumphed furiously. Doubtless his thoughts were transparent to her. "Don't suppose you have any of those delicious scones baked, like those you served at tea the other day?" He flashed her his most engaging smile.

Hannah was not to be charmed. "Get those at the bakery, my lord. Not much of a cook, really, though I make do. I was Miss Gwynneth's nurse, and when her mother died I came back to look after her." She folded her arms and turned a gimlet eye on him.

"And it's obvious you intend to continue doing an excellent job." Langley grinned and lowered himself into Mr. Dunlevvy's chair. "Gwynneth is her first name? Beautiful. What was she like as a little girl?"

Hannah warmed quickly to this subject, and Gwynneth found the two head-to-head, deep in conversation, when she emerged dressed in her riding habit, shako firmly fixed atop her braids. "I am ready, my lord."

But Hannah refused to let them leave until Gwynneth had had a bite of breakfast. "Your porridge will congeal, and you shouldn't go out riding without no nourishment at all, Miss Gwynny."

Gwynneth was always hungry in the morning, so she followed this sensible advice, while Lord Langley drank tea and chatted casually.

As Gwynneth ate her simple breakfast, Langley was free to study her closely. His eyes coursed the oval face and traced lovingly the faint trail of freckles across the bridge of her nose. Her small but beautifully shaped mouth closing on the spoon elicited a sharp hunger in him for something that wasn't porridge! A sigh escaped his lips. Yes, this was how "Miss Allen" should look—prim, proper, but with a promise of sensuality.

The sigh caused Gwynneth to glance up, and a blush spread over her cheeks at the look Langley was giving her. There was something in it that made her heart speed up so that she felt a little dizzy. To hide her confusion, she stood abruptly. "I am ready now, sir."

"Sure? I am in no hurry." But he rose, too, obviously eager to be off.

The morning mists were still lying along the low places

when they cleared the town. Because he wanted to speak to her with some degree of privacy, he steered her to the woods where they had met before, bidding his groom wait at the edge. Gwynneth uneasily followed him, but wouldn't go more than a few feet out of sight of the groom.

Irritated, Langley dismounted and held his arms up to her. "Come, Miss Dunlevvy. What I have to say concerns your safety, not your virtue."

Letting Pinky sidle away, Gwynneth regarded him gravely. "Sometimes they are the same thing, my lord."

"My word of honor, I won't touch you. Not even if you beg me to." A wicked gleam lit his eyes. "Unless you beg very persuasively."

"You mistake me very much if you think that I would ever . . ."

"Peace, Miss Dunlevvy. I wish to talk to you about Carter Grantham and the posthumous *Register*."

Reluctantly Gwynneth dismounted, slipping quickly from Langley's arms to put a distance between them. Why did the man affect her very breathing, simply by being near?

"What did Mr. Grantham have to say, Lord Langley. Did he think Sir Miles's charges were to be taken seriously?"

"Worse than that, I fear. He refused to involve himself in the situation. Did not think that you could be successfully defended." Langley's long face took on a grim aspect, the chiseled lines at either side of his mouth deep.

"Wh-why?"

"He believed you were lying about your involvement."

"Oh, no! I had a feeling that he didn't believe me, but . . ."

"Thing is, Miss Dunlevvy, Carter Grantham is a most perceptive observer of human behavior. He can read a blush, a sideward look, a hand gesture, like a book. He is almost always right in these matters." It was said sternly. She must think he was about to abandon her cause, so she would confess exactly what lie had caused her guilty looks. Then at last he could claim "Miss Allen."

Stricken, Gwynneth looked away, biting her lips. It was true. She had lied to Sir Carter, but not about her involvement with the newspaper. "I don't know what to say. Except that I didn't have anything to do with publishing that filth. I swear that I didn't. Perhaps if I could talk to Mr. Grantham privately . . ."

"I'm afraid that is impossible. He was quite put out with me for dragging him away from the victory celebrations in London, for what he regards as a disgusting, unwinnable case. He left for the city as soon as we returned to Nick's yesterday."

Gwynneth raised her eyes to meet Lord Langley's. He could see the struggle to decide written all over her face. Involuntarily he took a step forward and cupped the side of her face in his big hand. "Tell me all, Miss Dunlevvy. Let me be your friend."

A thrill raced through Gwynneth that set her whole being on fire. How very tempting it was to cast herself into his arms, sob out her story, and let him deal with her problems. But *he* was one of her problems—this wild feeling of desire that was racing through her would devour her if she gave into it. And if she gave in, she was ruined forever.

Taking a deep breath, Gwynneth pulled back, away from his tempting touch. "I *was* lying, in a sense, though Mr. Grantham is wrong about what the lie was."

A look of intense joy radiated from Langley. "I know you were, but we both know it has no bearing on your involvement in the posthumous *Register*, don't we?"

"Yes. As you realized immediately on reading it, the essay 'Market Day in Guilford,' which appeared in one of the early posthumous issues, was written by . . . by 'Miss Allen.' I was . . . I was protecting her."

"Protecting *her*!" It wasn't what he had been expecting

to hear, and certainly not what he had been wanting to hear. "Who exactly do you mean?"

"Why, Lady Ridgeway, of course. She must have given the essay to my father for some reason. He must have left it in his desk at the press, perhaps meaning to publish it some time when he had space. The person who published the posthumous issues found it and decided to print it. So can't you call Mr. Grantham back, or write him and explain?"

Langley was stung by her continuing lack of trust in him. So she meant to go on with the masquerade after all, eh? Even if it meant taking in his friend Carter, even if it meant endangering Lady Ridgeway? Baggage! All his desire for revenge returned, with an added force.

Firmly commanding his response, all he said was, in a very repressive voice, "I see. Of course. Or perhaps she is involved more deeply in the seditious, scurrilous publication. Do you think so, Miss Dunlevvy?"

"No, I am sure she is not. She would never . . ."

"Well, we will just have to see what Sir Miles comes up with, then. I hope the trail doesn't lead to her."

"I am sure it won't. If . . . if necessary, I will claim authorship of the piece."

"That is very decent of you, Miss Dunlevvy. You are as loyal as you are honest."

Langley's tone was so bitter, so ironic, that Gwynneth threw an alarmed look at him. "We'd best be getting back into sight of the groom, my lord."

"Oh, by all means. Your reputation, Miss Dunlevvy. Preserve it with your very life."

Again the bitter tone. Gwynneth wondered at it as he tossed her in the saddle and then mounted brusquely. What was up with him? With such a mercurial temperament, one never knew.

Solemnly they rode out of the forest and into the sunlight. Gwynneth was occupied with what measures she could take to protect herself against Sir Miles. Langley apparently didn't believe her; how else to explain his obvious disenchantment with her now, so she was on her own.

For his part, Lord Langley was once again plotting a dramatic way of forcing Gwynneth to reveal her identity and repaying her for leading him such a dance, when he heard her softly indrawn, "Oh, no!"

He looked up to see a party of riders approaching them. It appeared to be almost the entire Verleigh house party. Constance Blackwood hailed them gaily. "Yoohoo, Langley. Why didn't you wait for the rest of us. Such a marvelous morning for a ride."

The group was on them, and Gwynneth was surrounded before she could give in to the impulse to turn Pinky and gallop away.

Now that it was forced upon them, Langley was not sorry to have Gwynneth confronted with the need to meet his friends and acquaintances. It was time she got over this ridiculous notion of shutting herself off from society. He urbanely but determinedly introduced her to Miss Blackwood, Lady Trumbull, her daughter Elizabeth, and the Morleys. "And you've already met these rogues," he laughed, indicating John, Roger, and Nicholas.

Gwynneth nodded to each, her heart in her throat. Miss Blackwood was charmingly friendly, as was Lady Elizabeth.

Langley felt enormous satisfaction at this reception. But his pleasure was considerably lowered by the sight of Alana Morley's pinched face.

"Aren't you the bookstore Dunlevvy," the blonde asked in an indignant tone.

"Yes, Lady Morley, I am." Gwynneth straightened in the saddle.

Sir Alfred Morley urged his horse between his wife and Gwynneth, and leered at her. "Charming, charming. No wonder you have such a passion for country bookstores of a sudden, Langley."

"I . . . I must be going." Gwynneth gathered her reins and attempted to turn her horse.

"Nonsense, Miss Dunlevvy." Nicholas Verleigh spoke up, nervously eyeing Langley, who seemed stunned by the Morleys' behavior. "You must accompany us. We're going to ride up Trevor Brook to the waterfall, and then return to the house for a late breakfast."

"I am sure Miss Dunlevvy must needs look to her shop." Lady Trumbull's chins were quivering, her eyes blazing. "Come, Constance, Lord Dudley. Let us be the first over the gate." She put her spurs to her hunter's flanks and bounded away, followed immediately by Alana Morley and Roger.

"Will you come, Miss Dunlevvy?" Lady Elizabeth looked anxiously at Gwynneth. "We'd truly love to have you." Constance seconded her, and the remaining men joined in, Sir Alfred with more enthusiasm than Langley could like.

"No, I thank you. Lady Morley has the right of it. I must needs look to my shop." She turned a defiant glare on Langley. "No need to see me home, my lord. Your groom can accompany me, so that you can join your friends." She urged Pinky to be off, and even when Langley pulled alongside her, kept a fast, silent pace all the way back to town.

At her door he helped her down and whispered softly as he did so, "You should have gone with them, Miss Dunlevvy. There were more who were friendly than weren't."

"Yes. And I am sure the kind of friendship Morley offers is exactly what I could want." Gwynneth held herself very straight. "Thank you for your concern, Lord Langley. I shall manage somehow. If needs must, I shall apply to my relatives for assistance. However much they may wish it were not so, I am part of their family, and they will not wish to see a member of their family tried for sedition."

She offered him her hand; he took it and looked very sternly into her face.

"I will still stand your friend, Miss Dunlevvy. I never said that I wouldn't."

"No, but it was very clear you didn't believe me. Under that circumstance, I cannot place my trust in you. I bid you good day, my lord." She turned on her heel and entered the shop.

"You are a fine one to talk about trust," Langley muttered as he mounted Turk. "Well, I will show you where deception can lead you, and you won't like the lesson at all. But I won't abandon you to Sir Miles, no matter what."

Chapter Eighteen

When Langley entered the drawing room that evening before dinner, he found himself in the middle of a well-bred but very hostile battleground.

"Ah, there you are, Stuart. Everyone is at sixes and sevens because of you!" Alana Morley cast him a glance half-angry, half-triumphant.

He bowed to her. "My apologies, ma'am. What have I done to cause you pain?"

"You've introduced your lightskirt to us, my lord, that is what." Lady Trumbull's shrill accents set his teeth on edge.

"Nonsense," Nicholas insisted. "A fine young woman. Just because she's in trade don't mean . . ."

"In the woods alone with him, wasn't she. Not the thing, not the thing. And to think you expected my daughter and niece to further the acquaintance. Well, it won't happen. We are leaving tomorrow."

Constance Blackwood appealed to Langley. "Sir, I feel sure Miss Dunlevvy is no lightskirt. I can't believe you would introduce us to anyone who was not all that she should be. Please convince my aunt; I've no wish to leave now." She cast a shy but unmistakable look of adoration at Nicholas.

"Of course he'll affirm that she is all that is proper. But that don't make it so!" Lady Trumbull quivered with indignation, just as if she hadn't spent the last several weeks in the bed of another woman's husband.

"Yes, I will, because she is. We were accompanied by a groom, and . . ."

"We know that, Lord Langley. It was the sight of your groom pacing at the edge of the woods that led us to ride in that direction in the first place." Alana almost purred the words. "He was clearly visible, but you and Miss Dunlevvy were nowhere to be seen as we approached."

"They came riding out almost immediately," Nicholas anxiously assured her. "I've told you Lord Langley had some important private business to discuss with her. But I am sure the groom could see them."

"Ha!" Lady Trumbull snorted.

"Miss Dunlevvy and I were not ten feet from the clearing. Our groom could see us at all times, I assure you. Miss Dunlevvy is quite fair; I wished her to be shielded from the sun while we discussed our, ah, business."

"Even if that much is true, why did you invite her to go along with us, Mr. Verleigh? And to join us here afterward for breakfast? A shopkeeper! I don't believe in mixing the classes. Not at all the thing." Lady Trumbull shook her plumed head vigorously. "I know Constance's parents would not wish her to be associating with such riffraff."

"Mother, Miss Dunlevvy is not riffraff. She is the former Earl of Fenswicke's granddaughter." Lady Elizabeth added her plea.

"And a shopkeeper!" Lady Trumbull was unswayed.

"A most delectable-looking shopkeeper, I must say," Morley observed. "I say, Langley, if you haven't an interest there, perhaps . . ."

"She is a respectable female, I repeat. Anyone who insults her will answer to me." Langley's low-voiced threat stopped Sir Alfred in mid-sentence.

John McDougal strove to make peace. "Now, Lady Trumbull, dinnae fash yersel! No harm has been done. Miss Dunlevvy wisely declined to join us, after all. Surely you can stay until the hunt and ball? I know Miss Blackwood has been looking forward to it, as has Lady Elizabeth." He glanced fondly at that last-named young woman, who blushed and looked almost pretty as she gratefully agreed.

"Well, I suppose . . ."

"Of course we will. I'm sorry, Aunt, but I must insist. Do you return to London now it must be without me." Constance rarely asserted herself, but just now the diminutive brunet seemed very determined. At that moment the butler announced dinner, and with a sigh of relief Nicholas led the party into the dining room.

That night, very late, Nicholas, John, and Roger ran Stuart to earth in the library, where he was staring unseeing at the open pages of a book, his thoughts turned inward. He had many things to think over, not all of them pleasant. He realized that he hadn't taken seriously enough Gwynneth's belief that she would be ostracized for breaking society's rules. But it seemed as if merely keeping a shop was problem enough. The slightest hint of impropriety seemed all that was required to set her outside the pale entirely. It did not take a great deal of imagination to picture how she would be treated should she accept his ideas about living together without benefit of clergy.

"Ah, here you are, Stu. What did Miss Dunlevvy have to say about Carter's defection?"

"She was upset, of course. She denied lying, and I believe her." This last was for John and Roger's benefit. "She thinks her family might help her, if she is actually charged."

"Will they?" John settled himself in a chair across from Langley.

"You know them slightly, Nick. Would they?"

"Might. They could hardly want to see their family name disgraced. But on the other hand, they certainly turned their backs on the pair when Mr. Dunlevvy went into trade."

"Well, I for one am devilish glad you talked the Trumbulls into staying." The other three turned curiously to

John, who smiled self-consciously. "You see, lads, I am thinking of offering for Lady Elizabeth. Have reason to think her father may give his permission, no matter how much Lady Trumbull objects."

Astonishment reigned for a few moments. "Though you weren't in the petticoat line," Roger gasped. "Marriage. Pah! Leg-shackling. Not for us, eh, Stuart."

Langley looked at his avid disciple blankly. Before he could reply, Nicholas ventured, "Well, it's for me! I, too, plan to be married. Constance has accepted me, and though she hopes for her parents' approval, she is of age and doesn't have to have it. We plan to go to London after the hunt, see what they say. If they refuse, we'll be wed from here as soon as may be."

Stuart shook his head. "I can't believe this. Two of my best friends, caught in one summer. I pray you don't live to regret it. Nor your ladies either."

"I'd regret much more putting a woman I loved in a position to be chewed over by tabbies like Lady Trumbull the rest of her life. Not to mention being the subject of gallantries such as Morley offers!" Nicholas turned away from his friend in disgust. "Come, John, join me in billiards." He clapped McDougal on the shoulder.

"What rot! No need to get leg-shackled. Plenty of obliging females like Alana Morley around, what?" Roger chuckled, clearly expecting his mentor to agree with him. But Langley's face was contorted with some emotion that the younger peer did not recognize.

"A moment, Nick. I need to speak with Stu in private." John watched as the other two men took the hint and left, closing the door behind them.

Langley slammed his book shut and stalked to the window to stare out at the moonlight-drenched garden, a ferocious scowl on his face.

"One thought to offer you, lad, in case your blue devils

are more personal than just Nick and me deciding to marry."

Langley turned around to glare at the short Scotsman at his side. "Personal? What more personal than your two best friends planning to marry, thus enlisting two fine young women in legal slavery."

"May be a long shot, but I'm betting your interest in Miss Dunlevvy goes beyond merely an interest in freedom of the press."

"So?" Langley's tone and stance were belligerent.

"So remember how fiercely you came down on Roger for wanting to give up his title. Made the lad see how foolish it was for just one person to stand against society."

Brown eyes clashed with blue for a long moment before Langley looked away with a sigh. "Touché, John. But there's more to it that just a distaste for the institution, as you know."

"Aye. Y'think you'll be like your father."

"You can't deny I'm like him in many ways. My damnable temper . . ."

"Is not like his at all. The old baron nursed his ills until he exploded, and then took some drastic action. And once he'd made up his mind to it, he'd never back down."

"You do not need to remind me. My mother suffered greatly as a result of his implacability. Do you think I'd take the chance I might experience the power I'd have over a wife in just such a way? Fact is, the more I feel for a woman, the less do I dare wed her."

"Whist, mon. Your temper is not like his at all. 'Tis a great deal more like your mother's—very hot to hand but quick to cool. And you are the opposite of implacable. Mercurial is more like it. And I've known you man and boy, these twenty years, so I know whereof I speak."

Langley grasped his friend by the shoulders. "You truly think I'd not act as he did?"

"I know not."

Relief softened Langley's stern features. "If you're right . . ." Musing, he stared out into the moon-drenched garden while McDougal waited. With sorrow the Scotsman watched Langley's hands gradually close into fists again.

"But if you're wrong . . . how could I ask the woman I love to take such a terrible risk?" He shoved open the French doors on the terrace and stalked out into the night.

I nearly told him. Gwynneth marveled over her close call as she dashed up the stairs to change out of her riding dress. *Madness, madness. The way he makes me feel when he touches me—and he's not even very interested in me now. If he were to really exert himself to seduce me . . .*

Gwynneth knew that if Lord Langley learned she was the much admired Miss Allen, he would bend all his charm and powers of persuasion upon her. She did not deceive herself as to her vulnerability to the man. Though inexperienced, she was not unaware of the power of desire to overcome the most determined virtue. And even if she could manage to stand firm, would he respect her refusal?

The way he had behaved that first day still stained her view of him. Though she no longer believed him a complete villain, she saw him as a man given to strong emotions, and prone to act on them even though he might repent later.

Hannah clucked over her as she helped her change. "Never should have gone with that man. Look at the taking you be in. Anyone can see he's a rogue."

"You seemed to be having a comfortable coze with him while I was dressing this morning," Gwynneth retorted.

"Aye, well, he's a charming rogue, but a rogue for a' that. Best not have anything to do with these fine gent'men, Miss Gwynny. They can mean only trouble to you now, lass."

Just then there was a knock on the door, and Mr. Highley informed Gwynneth that Sir Miles Barlow wished to speak with her in her office. She cast an arch look at her old nurse. "The problem is, Hannah, the 'fine gent'men' insist on having something to do with me!"

Smoothing on her oldest and least attractive black bombazine dress and covering her braids with her ugliest cap, Gwynneth descended to her office to find Barlow going through her desk.

"Sir Miles. How may I assist you?" She made her voice as cold and depressive as she could.

"Ah, Miss Dunlevvy." Showing not the least dismay at having been caught going through her papers, Sir Miles turned and raised a quizzing glass. After inspecting her thoroughly while she stood rigid and furious, he took out a snuff container and delicately inhaled a pinch. "That outfit does not flatter you, my dear."

"If you please, sir, I have much to do."

"Poor Miss Dunlevvy, condemned to such somber raiment. But did I not see you in lavender a few days ago? Could it be that this lovely exercise in *corbeau* is for my benefit?"

"You flatter yourself, sir." Gwynneth advanced on him determinedly and gathered the papers he had been perusing, which turned out to be a collection of statements she had been preparing to send to customers. "Please state your business or leave me to do my work."

"Very well, my business is simple. Are these papers written in your own hand?"

Gwynneth looked from the desk to Sir Miles's assessing stare. Why did he wish to know that? "Yes, they are. Would you explain . . ."

"All in good time. I need a sample of your handwriting. May I?" He selected one of the longer statements and folded it.

"Let me see that. No, please don't take that one. It took me quite an hour to compile that bill. Here." She rummaged through her desk and found a note she had written to remind Mr. Highley to order coal. "Will this do?"

Sir Miles raised his quizzing glass and studied the note. A slow, malevolent smile stretched his full lips. "Perfect. Much better, in fact. I thank you, Miss Dunlevvy. I will leave you to get on with your day's work, but may I suggest that you put your affairs here in good order? I expect you will be accompanying me to London shortly."

"London!" Gwynneth gasped. "With you to London? I most certainly will not. You must be mad, sir."

"Not mad, though I may become angry if you continue to take this unfriendly tone with me. You will be given a choice of going to London as *my* guest or the government's. Believe me, you will enjoy *my* hospitality much more!" He tried to take her hand. She shrank back, head high and chin jutting obstinately.

"Perverse creature. Shall I describe to you the treatment that pretty females receive in Newgate, Miss Dunlevvy? Friendless pretty females, in particular. I am told that one who escapes being raped above a dozen times her first day there must count herself fortunate."

Her breath hissed between her teeth at his shocking words. "This is England, sir, where justice prevails . . ."

"Ah, yes. But justice takes time, and often requires money to move at all. Time that you will not want to spend in Newgate. Money that you may find difficulty in acquiring. Which is why I suggest you take a much more conciliatory tone to me. I would be willing to assist you for certain, ah, considerations."

Once more he tried to take her hand, but Gwynneth retreated from him in panic, her eyes wide with horror.

"I will give you a little more time, golden eyes, to change your manner with me. But only a little. My work here is almost done." He took his cane, made her an elaborate, ironic leg, and sauntered past Highley, who had been observing all that transpired from the door between her office and the shop.

Both were silent until Barlow had closed the front door. Then Highley rushed toward her. "Miss Dunlevvy—Gwynneth—I fear you are in grave danger. You must send a note to your friends right away."

Gwynneth dropped into her chair and slumped dejectedly. "I have no friends, Ezekial. I fell out with Lord Langley today. His legal adviser, Mr. Grantham, did not believe that I was not involved in the posthumous publication of the *Register*."

"What shall you do, then?"

"I don't know. I can't think. Perhaps . . . perhaps Lady Ridgeway can suggest someone."

Highley let out a snort that told what he thought of that forlorn hope, but Gwynneth did not know who else to ask. Though she had told Langley her relatives might help, she doubted it very much, and indeed her pride would scarcely permit her to apply to them. Besides, from the way Barlow talked, she did not have time to write them and wait for an answer.

So she penned a note to Lady Ridgeway, asking her for a brief audience. Donning a wide-brimmed old straw bonnet, she made the thirty-minute walk to Lord Ridgeway's Tudor country home with little hope in her heart.

To her pleased surprise, Lady Ridgeway agreed to see her immediately, and was most cordial. "This is nonsense," she snapped, when told of Barlow's charges and threats. "Told him so myself. I will give you a note to take to my solicitor in Kendal. He can advise you. You must see him next Monday."

"Monday? I do not know if I have that long."

"Well, you can't see him before. I happen to know he is on the circuit now. My Arthur has business with him, too, and he wrote us he would not be available before July fifteenth."

"I had the impression Sir Miles intended to arrest me right away."

Lady Ridgeway thought quickly. "I daresay I can delay him a bit. He's putting up at the inn. I'll invite him here, and convince him to attend Verleigh's hunt and ball. That will keep him occupied through Saturday night.

"I'll try to talk to him about you, convince him you are not capable of scurrilous writing, and that you have powerful friends who will not be best pleased if you are arrested. And, my dear, you must contact your Fenswicke connections, no matter how it hurts your pride."

Reluctantly Gwynneth agreed to do so.

"To give you more time, we'll plan something to keep him here through the early part of next week. You can write your aunt and uncle, the young earl's guardians. They stand high with the government. Make no mistake, they'll help you, for his sake. Barlow's a toadeater, you know. Won't be able to resist being the guest of honor at a baron's dinner table, what? And when he hears from your Fenswicke relations, well . . ."

Gwynneth smiled. Lady Ridgeway was surprisingly acute in some ways. "I'm so grateful, my lady. I don't know what to say."

"Tut, girl. You've assisted my Virginia most ably. She and Langley get on quite swimmingly now. She's reading that *Odyssey* thing with him. He comes over every day for at least an hour to discuss it with her. Shouldn't be at all surprised if we don't have an interesting announcement soon."

Gwynneth suppressed pangs of chagrin and jealousy at this news. "If that is what Virginia wants, then I am very happy for her."

"Oh, she thinks him all that is wonderful."

A thankful, relieved Gwynneth took her leave of Lady Ridgeway and walked back to Guilford, musing on the way. The hunt and ball were Saturday. Langley had said he would return to London after that. She would then only have to worry about Sir Miles Barlow. With a friend like Lady Ridgeway on her side, perhaps she could prevail over him. How glad she would be to get back to the dull, uneventful existence that she had previously deplored, the existence that had been shattered the day the handsome Lord Langley had walked into her bookstore!

Sir Miles Barlow sat in his room at the White Hart Inn and contemplated the invitation in front of him. He had been about to gather up the delectable Miss Dunlevvy and leave town, but this promised to be diverting.

The truth was, he had been frustrated in his efforts to build a case against Langley and his friends that would connect them with the posthumous *Register*. Langley's only connection seemed to be through the slight friendship with Miss Dunlevvy, and after extensive questioning around town, he decided that the connection was too recent to hang a charge of libel and sedition on. Dudley and McDougal could not be linked to the newspaper at all. Nicholas Verleigh had certainly written for it while old Dunlevvy was alive, but Barlow's best efforts had been unable to show any link with the posthumous editions.

He had been more successful in linking Miss Dunlevvy to the paper. Not that the Irish pressman had implicated her, as Barlow had led her to believe. No, that fiery-haired and fiery-tempered young man apparently had the ambition to be a martyr to the cause of freedom of the press, and so had refused even under very considerable pressure to reveal any of his confederates.

However, a search of his quarters had turned up a fair copy of an essay on market day in Guilford that had been published in the first edition of the posthumous *Register*. It was in a distinctive feminine hand, quite unlike the Irishman's crabbed scrawl. Quite unlike his style, too. It was a stroke of genius, Sir Miles told himself, to compare it with

Miss Dunlevvy's handwriting. Now he had her, pretty little bird, right in his hand.

Not that Sir Miles believed her guilty. He was as able as Lord Langley to read the purpose of the heavy drapes over the windows at the press, and of the elaborate efforts to remove all evidence of the posthumous *Register* from the premises. Nor had the fact that the *Register* was circulated only in London rather than on its home ground escaped him.

And even if Miss Dunlevvy had the will to write such libelous, scurrilous things, he doubted she had the experience or vocabulary. Clearly the Irishman was using her press without her knowledge. No, she was an innocent, but she was not to know that he believed that, or that he knew his case against her was far too flimsy to take to court.

In spite of the brave, defiant front she put on, she would be terrified at being arrested, and would hasten to accept his generous offer of assistance in return for her favors. If she did not, a night or two in Newgate would doubtless convince her.

What a triumph it would be to flaunt her before Langley, who clearly desired the chit. She was no diamond, true, but pretty enough, with both fire and breeding, just the sort both he and Langley admired. For once he was going to win over Stuart Hamilton, and how sweet victory would be!

Sir Miles Barlow did not ordinarily keep a mistress—his pockets were not plump enough for a highflier. But Gwynneth Dunlevvy would cost him little more than the price of cheap lodgings and a few gowns. Unlike the usual lady bird, she would have no reason to expect jewels or money. Her favors were to be paid for with her freedom. When he tired of her, and of humiliating and irritating Langley, he would let her go. No need to pension her off or give her a parting gift, either. All in all, a highly satisfactory arrangement.

If he accepted the invitation from Lady Ridgeway, it

would delay by a few days his enjoyment of Miss Dun-levvy's surrender. But it would give him the opportunity to rub shoulders with some not inconsequential members of the *ton*. And the Ridgeways had two marriageable daughters, doubtless with respectable dowries. To further an acquaintance like that, which held out the possibility of an advantageous match, he would gladly delay his rendezvous with Miss Dunlevvy for a short while.

And since Langley would be at the ball, he would enjoy the opportunity of twisting the baron's tail over the girl, too. He would leak enough to convince Langley that she was already in his power, and watch the man squirm.

Oh, yes. Well worth the brief delay! Sir Miles picked up a quill and began to write a gracious acceptance to Lady Ridgeway.

Chapter Nineteen

After his midnight stroll, Lord Langley decamped. A cryptic note assured Nicholas that he would be back in time for the hunt ball, perhaps in time for the hunt. As he had taken neither valet nor carriage, Nicholas assumed he could not have gone far, and set himself to smoothing the still-ruffled feathers of some of his guests, especially Lady Trumbull, to insure that Miss Blackwood remained with him until after the ball.

Kendal's oldest solicitor stared at Lord Langley after that worthy had explained his wishes. "Surely, my lord, you cannot mean this. Such a document would make the woman completely independent of you."

"That is entirely what I wish."

"But it means, if she chose not to live with you . . ."

"Exactly. She would have a choice."

"And she would have a legal claim to custody of any children."

"You understand me precisely."

"No, my lord, I understand your instructions, but I do not understand you. Whether mistress or wife, if woman is not subject to man, she is capable of any number of freaks and starts. It is against the order of nature."

"Nevertheless, you can draw up such a document?"

"Assuredly."

"Immediately. I wish to take it with me today."

The old man shook his head. "With the necessary copies,

my lord, even if I set both clerks to work overnight, tomorrow morning at the earliest."

"Tomorrow morning, then, and I will compensate you all warmly for your extra effort."

The solicitor stood and bowed his distinguished guest out of his office, shaking his head at the foibles of the aristocracy.

Gwynneth knew she couldn't hear the huntsman's horn or the baying of the hounds from her shop, yet a dozen times Saturday it seemed to her that she could, and she raised her head to listen, but heard nothing other than the anxious pounding of her own heart. It had been a nervous few days, every moment dreading the appearance of Sir Miles Barlow, every moment yearning for the appearance of Lord Langley, in spite of herself.

She was restless and alert that day, as if threatened by some unknown danger. When she heard the shop door bang open, the agitated shout of Lord Langley, "Where is she, I must see Miss Dunlevvy immediately," it was as if she had been expecting it all day. But she was unprepared for the awful look on Langley's face.

He had evidently come straight from the hunt, for he was dressed in dirt-spattered and disheveled riding clothes. Highley stood irresolutely by the door until she nodded to him to leave them. "What is it, Lord Langley?" she asked in alarm as the door to her office closed behind them.

"That great beast, that brute, that drunken bastard of a husband. I should have just shot him like a dog."

"What happened?"

"I could call him out." Langley tore his hair and paced the room, dwarfing it and filling it with his restless energy.

"Please, Lord Langley. Calm yourself and tell me . . ."

"But if he killed me, she'd be at his mercy, and I hear Ridgeway's a good shot."

"If you'd only tell me . . ."

He turned to her and grasped her by the shoulders, a wild, crazed look on his face. "I'll take her away. We'll elope. That's the only way."

"Now, Lord Langley, *please*. Calm yourself. Lady Ridgeway won't elope with you."

"She will. She must. I don't intend to give her any more choice. I can't leave a woman like her at the mercy of that soul-destroying brute. If she won't go with me willingly, I will abduct her."

Gwynneth gasped. "No, Lord Langley. You mustn't. Please sit down and calm yourself."

"No!" He fairly roared at her. "My mind is made up. We'll elope, go to Italy. She will love it. We can be happy there. No more platonic friendship, either. I've always suspected 'Miss Allen' was meant to be my life's mate. Now I mean to claim what is, what should be mine! Tell her to be prepared to leave with me from the ball tonight."

He started for the door. Gwynneth threw herself after him, grabbing his shoulder and pulling him around. "You're mad! She won't go willingly. You can't abduct Lady Ridgeway."

"I can and I will. You, Miss Dunlevvy, are to go to her right now. Tell her my carriage will be waiting at the end of Mr. Verleigh's drive, a fresh, fast team in the traces. She can leave the hunt ball and come to me. I'll wait till midnight and then if she hasn't joined me voluntarily, I *will* come and get her. I'll have several armed men with me, and we'll take her by force."

"No!" Gwynneth screamed. "You can't. I have to talk to you. There is something I must . . ."

"The time for talk is over. Take the message, Miss Dunlevvy." With that, Lord Langley flung her away and raced out of the room. He was out of the shop door before she could stop him, and mounted and rode away in spite of her agitated call for him to stop, which made several people on the street stare at her.

Oh, what could have happened to set him off that way? Gwynneth paced her office in a panic. The ball would begin soon. She had to do something. She had to stop Lord Langley from abducting Lady Ridgeway. Never had she intended any harm to come to the woman, and especially not now that she was deeply indebted to her for helping keep Barlow at bay. What a terrible repayment it would be, to involve her in a scandal that would make her an *on-dit* throughout society and very likely destroy her marriage.

There was only one way, Gwynneth realized. Now, she would have to reveal herself to Lord Langley. She had tried to when he began raving about abducting the baroness, but he had been too full of rage to pay attention to her. Somehow he must be made to listen. He'd be so angry, she quailed from the thought of it. But there was no other way.

She'd have to intercept him, find a way to speak to him. The thought of going to the ball horrified her—all those eyes . . . and his anger might well make the whole matter public.

So she must go to his carriage and wait for him there. The thought made her shudder. To do that would be to put herself completely in that unpredictable man's power.

Gwynneth paced up and down, trying to think of another way. Perhaps a letter? But if it went astray? Or he didn't believe it?

And what if he didn't believe her anyway? Gwynneth realized she'd have to prove her story to him somehow. After spending so much time seconding him in his belief that 'Miss Allen' was Lady Ridgeway, she suspected she would have some difficulty disabusing him of the notion.

At last she decided what she must do. She asked a worried Hannah to lay out her new spring-green crepe de chine dress, wishing she'd had time to complete the fichu of lace she'd been planning to fasten to its low-cut neckline. The rather revealing dress was not the best choice for dealing with a man of Langleys' temperament, especially in an explosive situation such as this.

But there was no time for regrets or hesitation. She ran downstairs and caught Mr. Highley locking up.

"Get me a hackney, please, Ezekial."

He looked at her in astonishment. "You're going out, miss?"

"I'm going to the hunt ball. I-I was invited, and I've decided to go."

Highley beamed. "I'm very glad to hear of it. But won't you need a chaperon? Or perhaps you could take Hannah?"

"No, I'll make do. After all, I'm not just out of the schoolroom."

"But . . ."

"No, please don't argue with me, Ezekial. Just get the cab."

Mr. Highley recognized that tone of voice. Gwynneth was normally the gentlest and most indulgent of employers, but there could be steel in her on occasion.

He left on his mission, and Gwynneth went into her office to pack a small portable writing desk, complete with ink and quills, of the kind that they sold to travelers, along with several copies of her poems. If nothing else would convince him, she would demonstrate her handwriting before his eyes.

This done, she returned upstairs to give further thought to her toilet. Hannah assisted her into the silk dress and rebraided her hair, weaving it in a crown around her head. Gwynneth fastened her mother's pearls in her ears and around her neck. Finally, she wrapped a fine ivory Norwich shawl around her shoulders, not because of any chill in the warm summer night, but to hide the décolletage of her dress.

The hackney arrived at last, drawn by a slow, spavined horse. It looked impossibly out of place moving down the rows of fine carriages to deliver her to Mr. Verleigh's door.

Her original hastily formed plan had been to slip into Lord Langley's carriage to await him there, but on further reflection, she had realized that he might keep Lady Ridgeway in sight at the ball, and if his intended quarry never left, he mightn't leave himself until he'd put into action whatever plan of abduction he might have.

Part of her wondered if he would truly do so rash a thing, but then she remembered the crazed look on his face this afternoon. She remembered, too, what he had said to her that day at the end of their ride. He had abjured her to inform him if Lady Ridgeway ever needed him. "I would risk *all* for her," he had said, and she had believed him.

Her belief in his determination was underscored as they passed down the drive, for there, nearest the gates, was Lord Langley's carriage, his arms emblazoned on the door, and a fine team in the traces, though other guests' teams were unhitched and were being walked by their grooms. Why would he, as Verleigh's houseguest, need a carriage at the ready unless he was planning to depart, and quickly, from the looks of the hitched team?

So it was that Gwynneth, uninvited by her host, climbed the stairs toward the Verleigh hunt ball. She wasn't really afraid of being turned away. A hunt and its ball were relatively democratic in this part of the country; those who could mount themselves adequately were welcome to follow the hounds, and those who could dress themselves adequately would be welcomed into the ballroom.

Once inside, however, she knew she'd be the subject of talk, and more than likely of snubs, especially as she was unescorted and unchaperoned. But there was no help for it. Before the night was over, she might be seen entering Lord Langley's closed carriage—servants would see her if no others—so her reputation would be in ruins anyway if she failed in her mission at the ball.

Still, she had no choice; she couldn't let Lady Ridgeway's life be ruined when she was innocent of any knowledge of Gwynneth's deception.

Gwynneth blinked a little at the brightness inside Verleigh's mansion. Candles blazed from myriad candelabra and chandeliers, their reflections sparkling in mirrors and highly polished marble floors. The crowd spilled out of the ballroom into the entrance hall, so that curious eyes followed her from the moment she entered as she made her way toward the ballroom doors, seeking Lord Langley.

She hoped to avoid going to his carriage if at all possible. Perhaps she could persuade him to go into a quiet room with her, here in the mansion. The library, perhaps? There she could convince him, even demonstrate her writing to him if necessary to prove her identity as "Miss Allen."

Suddenly he swooped down on her as if conjured by her thoughts. Gwynneth's nerves nearly failed her. The man towered over her, looking angry and menacing. "Miss Dunlevvy. You here?" He pulled her aside, glaring furiously. It was not an auspicious greeting. "Why? Have you delivered my message?"

"Lord Langley, could I speak with you for a moment?"

"Of course." He took the portfolio containing the writing desk from her hand before she could resist. "They're playing a waltz. We can talk as we dance." With an imperious lift of his eyebrow he summoned a footman and handed her things to him. She tried to retain the shawl, but he drew it off her shoulders, a knowing grin suddenly relieving the serious look on his face.

In evening dress Lord Langley was an imposing figure. He had abandoned his comfortable, unfashionably loose clothing for an impeccably fitted masterpiece of the tailor's art. The form-hugging black coat and black silk knee britches were set off by an intricately embroidered wine on gray waistcoat and a snowy, elaborately arranged neck cloth in which was tucked a single ruby. Gwynneth felt quite breathless at the handsome picture he presented.

There was a strange light in his eyes as he drew the awed young woman through the ballroom doors and into his arms. "Under other circumstances I would relish this opportunity as it deserves," he asserted, brown eyes caressing her person all too appreciatively.

As would I, Gwynneth thought, almost overpowered by his nearness and the feel of his warm, strong hand on her waist.

He spun her onto the floor and into the swirling crowd of waltzing dancers with consummate skill. "But I am so eager to hear what my darling has said. Is she willing? Eager, perhaps? Did you tell her about Italy?"

"Lord Langley, I need to talk to you privately, to show you something, before . . ."

"No, Miss Dunlevvy. Do not think to talk me out of this. If Lady Ridgeway has any more stratagems, tell her for me that I won't take no for an answer."

So saying, Lord Langley executed a series of close, quick turns that left Gwynneth breathless and disoriented. Their movements brought her body briefly into full contact with his long, muscular frame, and she felt her heart leap like a frightened deer. By the time she had gotten herself under control, the music was ending. Langley bowed to her. The expression on his face was hard with determination.

"Go, Miss Dunlevvy. Tell her now what I have said. No stratagems, no pretty arguments by you or cleverly worded letters by her. After this afternoon, I feel entirely justified in taking matters into my own hands. I'll watch you to see that you tell her what I have said. There she is, cool as you please with the chaperones. Would you believe she refused to dance with me with a coy little laugh. Why, I could almost believe you hadn't delivered my message at all. Go now, Miss Dunlevvy."

Chapter Twenty

Lord Langley gave Gwynneth a little shove in the back with his gloved hand, and she knew she must return to her original plan, even though it would result in putting her completely at his mercy in a closed carriage. Would he beat her, or make love to her? Or both? Gwynneth suppressed a shudder of apprehension as she approached Lady Ridgeway, who turned to her with a surprised look.

"Why, Miss Dunlevvy. I never expected you to be here at the ball."

Gwynneth pasted a smile on her face. "Lord Langley prevailed upon me to attend."

"Lord Langley. Oh, do not speak to me of that man." Lady Ridgeway looked anxiously past Gwynneth's shoulder to where Langley lounged against a doorpost, watching the proceedings with a look of sardonic amusement. "If you ask me, he is a bit queer in the attic!"

Just then Lady Ridgeway's daughter was returned to her by her partner. Virginia greeted Gwynneth enthusiastically. "Miss Dunlevvy! How lovely to see you here. I saw you dancing with Lord Langley. Isn't he the most fabulous dancer!"

"Indeed, quite breathtaking."

"He has asked for two dances. Mother would only allow him one." Virginia pouted prettily at her mother, who shushed her chick and steered her toward her new partner.

"Not sure he's right for the gel, Miss Dunlevvy. Excitable fellow, behaved rather oddly today."

Since Gwynneth could well believe that Lord Langley's behavior would seem odd to Lady Ridgeway, she murmured something soothing. She hoped the baroness would reveal what had happened this day to upset Langley so, but her curiosity went unsatisfied. Instead, Lady Ridgeway dismissed him petulantly.

"Rather too bookish, also. And those radical notions of his! Daresay I'd have a devil of a time getting Arthur to agree to him for a son-in-law."

Gwynneth felt she had talked long enough to convince Lord Langley that she had relayed his message. She could only hope Lady Ridgeway's irritable scowl would look to him like deep concern. "I must go, that is, I see a friend . . ."

"Take care, Miss Dunlevvy. Sir Miles is here. Did you write your relatives?"

Gwynneth nodded. Reluctantly she had taken Lady Ridgeway's advice, though she had little hope of the outcome. "They haven't responded yet, however. Did Barlow agree to stay with you a few days?"

"Oh, yes, rose to the bait like a trout to a fly. Think he has some notion of fixing his interest with Virginia, as if I'd let that mushroom marry my gel!"

Thanking her again for her assistance, Gwynneth took her leave of the lady and made her way around the ballroom toward where Langley still lounged, having to speak to several acquaintances and refuse an invitation to dance along the way. The curious looks and sly smiles she had been expecting could be seen on a few faces, but she was surprised at how cordial most of those who greeted her were. She grimly fought against any rekindled hope that the *ton* would accept her. After she met Lord Langley in his carriage, all would be lost, anyway.

Suddenly her way was blocked by her host and the

lovely blonde who had been in her bookstore with Lord Langley that day, and who had so firmly snubbed her the last time she went riding with him. "Miss Dunlevvy, so very pleased you have come." Nicholas Verleigh bowed to her, and she could detect nothing ironic in his manner. Indeed, he did not even seem surprised to see her.

"May I present Lady Morley, Miss Dunlevvy?" Gwynneth turned and reluctantly met the vivid blue eyes that were studying her avidly. She held out her hand, and Lady Morley offered her, very briefly, two fingers.

"Actually, we've been introduced before, haven't we? Charmed. These country balls, so democratic. Your waltz with Lord Langley was much, ah, admired." The cultured voice dripped sarcasm.

Gwynneth felt the color mounting her cheeks. "He dances very well" was all she offered.

"Indeed, as I well know. And so like Stuart with his leveling notions to single out a shopkeeper . . ."

"Here's your partner, Alana, come to claim you for the next dance." Verleigh cut across his guest's deliberately spiteful remarks firmly. "May I have the pleasure, Miss Dunlevvy? They are forming sets for a country-dance."

Gwynneth bit her lower lip. Mr. Verleigh was clearly embarrassed by his guest's hostility and wished to make amends. But she had been distracted long enough from her mission. "Thank you, but I cannot. I must speak to someone, and then I must leave, as I have a hackney coach waiting."

To her relief, Verleigh permitted her to escape with only a murmur of regret.

Lady Morley was not the only one who had observed Langley's dance with Miss Dunlevvy with a jaundiced eye. Sir Miles Barlow had not been expecting her at the hunt ball, though Lady Ridgeway had made it clear the girl was well regarded in the county. He was not at all pleased to see her dance with Langley, but the way his rival looked at the chit made his plans for her all the more appealing. Langley could hardly take his eyes off her. *How vexed he will be when he learns she is as good as my mistress.* Barlow could not resist the temptation to gloat, so he approached his rival as Langley's eyes followed Gwynneth's progress across the room.

"Golden eyes is looking exceptionally fine tonight, isn't she, Stuart."

Langley gave a start; he had been concentrating on Gwynneth so much, he was unaware of the other man's approach. "I presume you mean Miss Dunlevvy. Yes, she looks most fetching in that green."

"I must arrange to have a dance with her later. Though I shall have plenty of her company in a few days."

Casually Sir Miles took out his snuffbox and sniffed a dainty helping from the back of his wrist, gleefully aware that he now had Langley's full attention.

"Just what do you mean by that, Miles?"

"I mean that I have succeeded in linking her to the publication of that scurrilous rag, and she will soon be under arrest—unless, of course, she offers me some, ah, inducement not to do so."

"Miss Dunlevvy would never . . ."

"Which she more than hinted she would do. Amazing how seductive an innocent-looking woman can become when she is frightened."

"You pig! You'll never lay a hand on her! You'll have to answer to me if you do."

Barlow chuckled. "Ah, Stuart. When will you learn that the age of the all-powerful aristocrat is drawing to a close. The law is my master—and yours."

"The law does not permit you to use it to threaten innocent young females into your bed."

"By the time the matter could come before any court, she will no longer be innocent."

"I warn you, Miles, if you harm her, you'll answer to me!"

"You don't frighten me, Stuart. I have powerful friends . . ."

"I doubt if you have even one true friend, whereas Miss Dunlevvy has many. Not to mention myself, Nicholas, and Lord Dudley. There are also her relatives. The Earl of Fenswicke's guardians have been applied to. They will not stand idly by while you ruin his cousin." The music had stopped, and the swirling couples were drifting their way.

"We can finish this discussion in a more appropriate place, I am sure." Barlow was sweating. He now regretted having tipped his hand to Langley; heretofore he had doubted Miss Dunlevvy's relatives would assist her, but if someone as prominent as Lord Langley had applied to them, they might bestir themselves.

He saw that he would have to act more quickly than he had planned if he hoped to carry off Miss Dunlevvy. Her relatives would forget they ever knew her, of course, once her ruin was a fait accompli. He gave Langley a bow and walked away, hoping he looked more composed than he felt. Langley's intense response, though rather alarming, was deeply satisfying, and only made him the more determined to have Miss Dunlevvy. And once the chit had been his mistress, surely Langley wouldn't carry out his threat? It would be pointless, then, after all.

Barlow knew that carrying off Miss Dunlevvy would infuriate Lady Ridgeway. But Lord Ridgeway was very much a man after his own heart. If he could convince Ridgeway that Miss Dunlevvy was a dangerous radical, his arresting her might even increase his stature in the baron's eyes. In that case he could continue to court Virginia, no matter how her mother felt about him.

He decided to inform the Ridgeways that he must leave the next day. He would have Miss Dunlevvy arrested when she returned home after the ball. A night spent in Guilford's miserable jail could only assist her in deciding to bargain for her freedom.

When Gwynneth finally managed to reach Langley's side, she hastened into speech before her courage utterly failed her. "Lady Ridgeway will wait until you have left and then make her way to your carriage as soon as she can. Please await her within it. She was most insistent on that point."

Barlow's threats, far from deterring Lord Langley from his plans, convinced him more than ever that he was doing the right thing. Indeed, he must act quickly to forestall the wily snake. A wicked smile lit his features as he proceeded to carry out his masquerade. He took her hand and clasped it to his lips. "Thank you, Miss Dunlevvy," he breathed fervently. "I know she will not let me down. I will never forget the part you have played in bringing us together."

Gwynneth drew away with a shudder. Neither of them would ever forget this rather dark comedy of errors, she thought.

"Go then, Lord Langley. She won't attempt to leave until she knows you are actually in your carriage. Be patient. It may be awhile before she can escape without detection."

Lord Langley leaned down and whispered in her ear, "If she can't, my bully boys will come and help her, never fear." With a laugh, he sprang away from her and began pushing his way through the crowd.

Gwynneth followed him as best she could, but once again had to deal with acquaintances and would-be partners, so that she had lost sight of him by the time she reached the ballroom entrance. Some confusion followed before she could locate the footman who had taken her shawl and writing desk. When these were restored to her, she left the mansion, aware of curious eyes. It seemed to her that her ears burned with the comments being made.

Gwynneth at last completed the dim, flambeau-lighted gauntlet of carriages, coachmen, grooms, and footmen, to arrive at Lord Langley's carriage. His team was stamping in the traces and his footmen were alert at the coach's side. The coachman was already on the box. Furthermore, several armed outriders of fierce mien were mounted nearby. Clearly he had meant every word of his threat.

Gwynneth drew a deep, shuddering breath as she stared at Langley's coat of arms shining in gold and scarlet on the side of the gleaming black coach. Once she had entered that carriage with Lord Langley and the door closed shut on her, her reputation as a virtuous woman was at an end. The impassive footman who had moved forward to open the door for her would, she well knew, relish this tidbit of gossip over his pint of ale. The news would travel through Guilford like a fire in dry tinder.

She almost turned on her heels and hurried away. Let Lord Langley abduct Lady Ridgeway and discover his mistake too late. Let him face the consequences. It would serve him right for doing such an unprincipled, high-handed thing! But her conscience riveted her to the spot. Lady Ridgeway had done nothing to deserve her fate should he abduct her. Social ruin and the end of her marriage would surely result, and she wouldn't even have a lover to protect her, for Gwynneth was sure Langley would have little interest in Lady Ridgeway once he was convinced she was not "Miss Allen."

On leaden feet she walked toward her fate. The footman opened the door and helped her up the step, bowing her to her ruin.

In the dim light of the coach's interior lanterns, Langley was leaning toward her eagerly. His hand caught hers and drew her into the luxurious vehicle and onto the squabs beside him. Then . . .

"You!"

"I know you were expecting . . ."

"Lady Ridgeway, and by damn I'll have her and no more tricks." He took Gwynneth's shoulders roughly and turned her as if to thrust her back out the door, which had not yet closed. She almost dropped her portfolio struggling with him.

"Lord Langley, you must listen. I am 'Miss Allen.'"

"Gammon." He pressed her toward the door.

"I swear it." She wrenched herself from his hands and thrust the portfolio toward him. "I've brought proof. You must listen before you ruin an innocent woman's life and, incidentally, make yourself look very foolish."

Langley pushed the portfolio to one side, keeping his eyes on her face. "The foolish ones are you and Lady Ridgeway, to think you can pull this switch on me. And you! You'd risk anything for her, apparently. Such incredible loyalty. Exactly what has she done to earn it?"

"It's no switch. The only switch is the one you have made by concluding I am Lady Ridgeway, or rather, that she is me. You were deceived by the handwriting on the invitations."

He smiled at her, a pitying look on his face. "I was not deceived. 'Miss Allen' has a very distinctive handwriting, unique, ornate, but readable. When I saw it on the invitations, I knew at once that I'd found my beloved correspondent."

"Please listen to me! In actual fact, her ladyship has an abominable handwriting, and once deciphered, it is found to be full of the worst spelling errors to be imagined. As a result, she asks me to act as her amanuensis on formal occasions."

"That is preposterous. You are a very saucy young woman to try to carry this off. I saw her handwriting on a list of study questions she had made out for her daughter just a few days ago. You are not going to call that a 'formal occasion,' are you?"

Gwynneth shook her head. "I wrote out those questions for Virginia. Lady Ridgeway had not read the *Iliad* and didn't care to. Indeed, she appeared never to have heard of it."

"*You* wrote up those questions? Don't be ridiculous. Why would you do that? You aren't the girl's governess, or . . ."

"She asked me to. Look, I have brought a portfolio of my writing. It contains the rough drafts of many of my poems and . . ."

"Yes, that's what she told me, too."

"And I have come equipped to write something in front of you if that's what it takes . . . she told you what?"

"Well, Virginia told me so first, but I couldn't believe her, so I asked Lady Ridgeway."

"Lady Ridgeway told you that was my writing? When?" Gwynneth was astonished, not fully able to grasp the implications. Her hand, holding out the ink bottle, began to shake, and she thrust the container back into the portfolio.

Langley put back his head and eyed the coach's plushly covered ceiling as if in thought. "Ah, let me see, I believe it was last week sometime."

"But why . . . why did you still believe Lady Ridgeway is 'Miss Allen,' then?"

"She is lying, of course, as you are. Still hoping to keep her secret, the two of you pretend that you wrote the poems instead of merely acting as her amanuensis."

"Ohhh!" Gwynneth was near swooning. She had never thought of his putting *this* interpretation on matters.

"So if the bottle of ink is to prove that the poems are written in your hand, don't bother. It doesn't follow, you see, that you *composed* them. But perhaps you came prepared to compose a poem for me, Miss Dunlevvy? Something in Lady Ridgeway's style? I've no doubt you have something memorized for the occasion. The two of you are the most complete hands at intrigue, I must say." His face, stern and angry, Langley glared at her.

Gwynneth raised a trembling hand to her lips, stopping a

cry of dismay. This was terrible. Was there no way to convince him? Tears of frustration began to form as she stared hopelessly at the self-assured man seated beside her.

"Enough, Miss Dunlevvy. Are you at *point non plus*, my dear?"

"Yes," she wailed. "How can I prove it to you except by writing poetry right here and now, on a topic of your choosing?" She bit her lip. "But I've never felt less poetic." She fought back the tears.

He smiled then, and brought his hand up to caress the side of her face. "I'll not tease you further. You've gotten a little of your own back for teasing me so, but I don't want you to cry."

The warm, hard hand cradling the side of her head transfixed Gwynneth almost as thoroughly as his words. All she could do is stare at him, not quite comprehending.

He laughed outright. "I know you are my 'Miss Allen,' Gwynneth."

"You do? Thank heaven!" Her voice was tiny, barely a squeak. "For how long?"

"For certain? As I said, since the day I saw Virginia's study questions. Though I like to think I must have unconsciously known it before." His hand moved to touch a wisp of stray hair, to smooth it off her forehead.

"Since then!" Storm clouds began to gather in Gwynneth's eyes. She tried to toss her head free of his hand. "All this talk of abducting Lady Ridgeway . . . you were just bamming me."

He laughed delightedly. "Afraid so. Thought you needed a lesson, after the merry dance you've led me. Only fair you should have a little of your own back."

"How cruel you are. I have been half out of my mind!"

"No more cruel than you. Not only have you denied me the pleasure of knowing you, you have helped that lack-wit Virginia Ridgeway try to ensnare me. What if I had fallen into her trap? You would have let me marry such a creature, believing her to be an intelligent young woman, eager to learn."

"I wouldn't have let it come to that."

"I saw no evidence that you would speak out to prevent it. Instead, you maintained the masquerade, even in the face of the danger from Barlow."

"I fear I did not take Sir Miles as seriously as I should have, but . . ."

"And then, consider this. I didn't know if you would admit your identity if I confronted you. You might have contrived yet another lie, and I still wouldn't have known for sure. I had to smoke you out, to make you come to me and confess. If you suffered a little in the process, well, it was a suitable punishment, don't you think?"

Gwynneth sat very still, pondering his words. His hand rested on her neck, his thumb stroked her throat gently. The sensation was far too pleasurable. Looking down at her hands, Gwynneth asked in a low, emotion-choked voice, "And was it your intention all along to ruin me, as part of my punishment."

Langley drew back in astonishment. "How ruin you? I've hardly touched you. Not even taken a kiss." The hand moved to the back of her head, urging her toward him. His left hand lifted her chin. "Don't you think I deserve a kiss, at least?"

"You ruined me the minute I stepped into this closed carriage with you, and well you know it." Indignantly Gwynneth thrust away from him, eyes flashing.

"Closed carriage? But you are mistaken." Langley turned her again to face the door she had entered, and she saw to her complete and relieved astonishment that it was open and the poker-faced footman was standing at attention in a position where he could see all that went on inside. Moreover, just beyond him was a nattily dressed little man who had the look of a gentleman's gentleman, his arms folded and his gaze into the coach unwavering.

"You see, I've no more wish than you to be caught in a closed carriage with a virtuous female. I have no intention of marrying a chit merely because she maneuvers me into a compromising situation."

"Me, maneuver you?" Torn between indignation and relief, Gwynneth could manage only a half-choked laugh.

Langley smiled and settled back against the squabs. There was an appreciative glint in his eyes as he let them roam freely over her, dwelling for too long on the low neckline of her dress. He reached for her hand and pulled her gently but firmly nearer to him. "Would that I could manipulate you. I'd close the door and trot off with you in an instant. What do you say, my dear? My horses are at the ready. London or my country estate—your choice."

Chapter Twenty-one

L ord Langley's deep voice offering her carte blanche warmed her with its seductive intonation. It was what she had feared, yet somehow she was not afraid. The door to the carriage remained open, and Langley's words clearly recognized that she probably would not accept his offer. Gwynneth permitted herself the luxury of leaving her hand in his, though she gave her head a firm shake in response to his proposition.

Langley's thumb gently caressed her palm and ran along her wrist. Mesmerized, Gwynneth watched him as he peeled back her glove, then slowly and deliberately raised her hand and kissed it, his lips warm against her sensitive palm. When his mouth moved up her wrist, though, Gwynneth drew her hand away as from a fire. Indeed, a fire burned through her suddenly, and she knew her danger.

"No, I must go!" She turned toward the door, meaning to bolt, but he placed a restraining hand on her arm.

"No?"

She turned slowly and looked up into those dark eyes. Regret was there, and curiosity. "I wonder if you have any idea what you are saying no to, Gwynneth? I am not offering you merely carte blanche. What I offer you is so much more . . ."

"But not enough. Any more than Charles Osgood's offer of carte blanche was enough. I'll be no man's whore! Let me go." She struggled to put some distance between them.

"Whore! No!" Langley cleared his throat, shaking his head at the harsh word.

"Don't try to wrap any such relationship in fine linen. A woman who gives herself to a man with no thought of marriage, especially one who lets him 'take care of her,' is just that, a whore. She is a sinner and deserves to be shunned. I'd never survive the knowledge that I had let myself sink so low."

"So severe, so puritanical." His voice had a tender but amused quality to it as he tried to put his arms about her.

Thrusting him firmly away, she hissed at him, "Don't you understand, it would kill me! I might well give in to temptation but eventually it would destroy me."

He drew back and looked into her eyes a long time. Finally he seemed to come to some sort of resolution within himself and nodded his head.

"This is the fear that made you refuse to reveal your identity to me for so long, then?"

"Yes, my lord. My father made me swear never to reveal myself. He had good reason to fear you would offer me carte blanche, and from the tone of your letters I knew he was right."

There was a glint of anger in Langley's eyes. "Did it never occur to you that you could say no?"

"Of course. But I wasn't sure . . ." Gwynneth looked away, not quite meeting his eyes.

"You thought I would use force?" Astonishment warred with anger in the look he gave her.

Gwynneth defended herself hotly. "Well, our first meeting certainly did nothing to convince me otherwise!"

"I dare say you think that a home thrust, brat! Well, I admit my behavior was disagreeable, but if you will recall, at your refusal to kiss me I released you immediately." He paused, reflecting, then grinned ruefully. "Well, almost immediately."

Gwynneth was not amused. "You seemed a willful, unpredictable person, and I had no one to defend me."

"When you came here tonight, did you still fear I would use force?"

Gwynneth lowered her eyes. "I—I wasn't sure. I had begun to doubt it, but . . ."

"Then what were you so afraid of? that you would continue until the very last second the pretense that Lady Ridgeway was Miss Allen?"

She was mute. He lifted her chin with one finger, forcing her to look at him. "You were afraid of yourself. Afraid you'd want my lovemaking more than you want respectability." His eyes burned into hers.

"I . . . yes." Gwynneth's voice was almost inaudible.

"Ah, my adorable one." Triumph lightened his grave features. He drew her into his arms. "I tried to tell you I was offering more, but you wouldn't hear me. I want you to be my wife."

She stared at him, uncomprehending, for a long moment before exploding. "You do not!" All bristling indignation, she struggled free of him and once again tried to exit the carriage, only to be detained by a firm hand on her arm. She turned toward him. "Release me! How dare you mock me this way! If you mean marriage, why this elaborate scheme to half frighten me out of my wits over fear you would abduct Lady Ridgeway? And moments ago, you said you had no intention of being trapped."

"No more did I. I'll go of my own free will into parson's mousetrap. No one will trick me. And I wanted you to have the same choice. But you deserved some payback for the May game you made of me over Lady Ridgeway."

"You— You are insufferable. It was a cruel thing to do! I was half out of my mind with worry. And I can't believe you are so quickly converted into a proponent of matrimony. You are forgetting that I am indeed the woman you have corresponded with, on this very subject, in depth."

"No, I am not forgetting. I tried my ideas out on you even before I published my article in *The Legacy*, advocating a new sort of social contract between men and women, spelling out not only the terms of their union, but the terms of their parting, including support for the less affluent partner and shared custody of children."

"And you've always claimed monogamy, at least long-term monogamy, was unreasonable."

"That was before I came to know you, Gwynneth. I little dreamed there was a female whose mind I would admire so much. Now I find that in addition she has a charming person, a strong moral sense, and a deep loathing of the thought of being a social outcast."

"So you must know that we'll never suit."

He smiled confidently. "I know that I want you, and it seems plain I must marry you to have you. Moreover, I've known it all along, though I was reluctant to face it. It was clear in your letters, and the day you told me how devastated you were by Charles Osgood's offer. When I realized you and Miss Allen were one and the same, I knew what I must do.

"My position on marriage developed partly because I was determined never to put myself in that oh-so-tempting position of absolute power which husbands have in our insane society. I feared I would become just such a tryant as my father had been. I thought if once I could get you in my arms, I could change your mind."

He lifted her chin with a gentle finger, forcing her to see the arrogant self-assurance in his eyes. "And perhaps I could, as you have just now admitted. But I love you too much to try, knowing the price you would have to pay. So you have won our argument. We will be married!" He drew her back into his arms and began kissing her passionately.

The scent of him, the heat of his large body so near, the searing feel of his lips and hands moving on her, overwhelmed her senses. Gwynneth let herself drift into a wonderful golden land of sensuous pleasure, returning his kisses, permitting caresses she should repulse.

Langley drew away for a moment to gaze lovingly into her eyes. "It is as I knew it would be," he sighed. He glanced up and caught the eye of the grinning footman, and with a subtle, silent gesture ordered the door of the carriage closed.

Gwynneth lifted a languid hand to his face, caressing the firm jaw and then exploring with a tentative finger the vertical lines beside his mouth. "I've wanted to do that ever since I first laid eyes on you," she confessed. On a guttural sound of suppressed passion Langley lowered his head to kiss her again. She thrust her hand into his thick hair to urge him toward her.

The sound of a single horseman riding hard past the carriage ended their passionate embrace as the carriage team started and attempted to bolt, rocking the luxurious vehicle back and forth.

When the horses had calmed again, Langley smiled down at her and attempted to resume his passionate wooing. But Gwynneth had had a moment to allow sharp, painful reality to intrude on her reverie. "What can I be thinking of!"

She straightened her clothing and once again attempted to pull away from Langley. "I'm sure it would be unwise to marry a man who really doesn't want to be married, who'd marry only to satisfy his undoubtedly temporary passion."

Lord Langley was astonished and alarmed. It had never occurred to him that Gwynneth would not fall into his arms in grateful joy when he announced he would marry her. Nonplussed, hurt vibrating in his deep voice, Langley asked, "Don't you love me? Surely a little? I've been falling in love with you a little more with every letter we've exchanged."

She tried for a cool, dismissive tone. "Yes, Lord Langley, I expect I am at least a little in love with you, too. And the attraction between us cannot be doubted. But I am not at all sure it is the kind of lasting love that marriage can be based upon."

Softly, Stuart, he cautioned himself. She is both proud and stubborn. One misstep and you may lose her. Humbly he took her hand, looking the very pattern-card of misery. "Do you think you could at least call me Stuart."

She laughed in spite of herself. "Rogue. Don't come the pathetic with me!"

He smiled. "Then tell me what I must do to convince you that I love you, that I want you for all of our lives?"

Her eyes searched his anxiously. He appeared to be sincere. "How I do want to believe you." She cocked her head to one side. "Now that you know who I am, I suppose we must spend some time together."

She looked nervously toward the carriage door. "Oh! Not like this!" She moved along the seat to thrust it open again. His minions were still observing them, obviously with considerable interest. "Kindly do not close this door again," she snapped, and then perched on the edge of the seat like a bird about to take wing.

"Properly. With chaperones, I mean. We must get to know one another better, to see how we deal together. Your temper . . ."

"I know. I am irascible. And selfish. But truly, Gwynneth, I'm not violent."

Her eyes begged leave to doubt this. "And mercurial. One minute you are furious, the next, flirtatious, and the next, all disinterested kindness."

"And you are sensitive, easily wounded, and perhaps too fearful."

"Whereas you want a brave, strong woman."

"I want you."

"Then there is my social position."

He snorted in disgust.

"Don't laugh. It could be more important to you than you think, to be snubbed . . ."

"My darling, I am continually being snubbed for some sin or other, real or imagined. Marrying you would probably gain me more respectability than I ever wanted!"

"Perhaps." She couldn't help but respond to his impish grin. "Doubtless true. I could be the making of you."

He laughed out loud. "This is delightful. See how well we deal together already!" He attempted to draw her back into the circle of his arms, but she put her hands against his chest, forestalling him.

"But in all seriousness, I do wonder if I could fit into your world? I don't know, and in spite of what you think, neither do you. We need time to find out."

The dark eyes turned serious once more. "This is a very reasonable request, but I'm not sure we have time. Sir Miles Barlow is talking of arresting you. I don't know if it is a bluff or not, but if true, his plans for you are not at all honorable."

Gwynneth felt a shudder run through her. "I know. But I am to see Lady Ridgeway's solicitor on Monday, and I have written to my Fenswicke relatives. Surely they will assist me."

Holding both her hands in his, turning them this way and that, Langley considered. "If you think Lady Ridgeway would stand your friend . . ."

"I know she will. When I told her of his threats, she gave me the name of her solicitor. Also, she invited Sir Miles to stay with them for several days, to delay him from taking me to London."

"Damn. Excuse me, but I was hoping she could shelter you. But if he is there, it is out of the question."

"True, but I hope to hear from my aunt-in-law soon, and . . ."

"Too risky. After what he said tonight, you must go where he cannot easily lay his hands on you." The brown eyes were moving rapidly as if reviewing an unseen page. Gwynneth waited tensely as he thought.

"I know!" He gave her a quick, happy hug. "Let us see if Nicholas's sister can take you in. She is a very intelligent and spirited female. You will like her very much. We'll hide you there while I court you."

His eyes were full of such meaning her heart turned over, and she felt a restless warmth spread through her body. When he pulled her into his arms once more, she quite forgot the open carriage door and their interested audience. She sighed his name for the first time, thinking how wonderful it was to let her feelings for him flow unchecked. As they shared this wonderous embrace, she found herself admitting at last what she had for so long refused to acknowledge. She loved him. In spite of his uncertain temper and his radical views, in spite of his cruel tease over Lady Ridgeway, in spite of the uncertainty she felt over him as a husband, she loved him!

After a few ardent moments, it was Langley who pulled away, regretfully. "I think if I have any hope of preserving the proprieties with you, we must stop now. Let us return to the ball. We can begin our courtship there, and ask Nick to send a note to his sister." He motioned to the footman, who stepped forward to assist Gwynneth from the carriage.

"Does she live far from here?" The thought of Sir Miles made Gwynneth nervous.

"Very near. She is increasing, else she would be here tonight."

As they strolled down the line of carriages, heads together, planning their next few days, Nicholas Verleigh suddenly hailed them. They looked up to see him hurrying toward them.

"I was hoping you'd already departed. Lady Ridgeway is looking for you, Miss Dunlevvy. To warn you. For some reason Sir Miles has changed his mind about staying with her. He told her he was going to arrest you immediately and start for London."

Gwynneth sucked in her breath, panic assailing her.

"Don't worry, I won't let him near you." Langley wrapped a protective arm around her shoulder. "Nick, I was wondering if Sabrina could shelter Gwynneth for a few days. You see, she isn't quite ready to marry me, and . . ."

"Marry! By all that is holy, Stuart, what miracle is this?" Nicholas looked relieved and astonished at the same time.

"Yes, of course. You didn't think I'd insult the woman I love by offering her carte blanche, did you?"

Speechless, Nicholas could only stare at his old friend. Langley laughed. "Come, Nick, if I've managed to change my thinking, you can adjust to the change! About Sabrina?"

Nicholas had turned and was walking with them toward the brilliantly lit mansion. He appeared to be in deep thought. He stopped just before they stepped into the circle of light thrown down onto the marble steps. "No, Stu, it won't do."

"Your sister wouldn't want to be involved in such a low, sordid matter. I understand, Mr. Verleigh." Gwynneth drew herself up bravely.

"It isn't my sister. She'd stand buff. It's her husband. He's a good sort, but cautious and unimaginative, and devilish protective of her. He'd never allow it. Especially for a . . . a friend of Langley's."

"Easy, old man. I told you . . ."

"I know, Stu, and I believe you. If I doubted your honorable intentions, I wouldn't doubt Miss Dunlevvy's—not at all surprised she didn't dash off with you tonight. But Westcott won't want Sabrina to experience the least worry or distress, which she would be bound to do, should Barlow show up there demanding Miss Dunlevvy."

Nicholas was obviously agitated. "But what's to do? She can't return to the ball. I know when Miles saw that Miss Dunlevvy had left, he sent a footman dashing off into the night. I can only guess it was to alert his soldiers to arrest her at her home. If he sees she is still here . . ."

"Doubtless that was the rider who dashed by us a few minutes ago." Stuart ran his hand through his hair distractedly, then took Gwynneth's hands and turned her toward him. "I can't let him near you, Gwynneth. This settles it, my love. He'd never dare to arrest the wife of a peer. Most particularly not *my* wife, for he would know he'd never live to tell the tale."

At her uneasy movement Langley seized her by both arms and gave her a little shake. "Gwynneth, you love me. If you don't know it now, you soon will. And I adore you. It is but a short dash to the Scottish border from here, and my carriage is at the ready. Thanks to Nick's reluctant cooperation in my little bit of stage setting, we even have armed outriders standing by. We're eloping."

Giving her no time to reply, he shook his friend's hand and, turning, began to half drag, half run her back to the carriage.

He bundled her inside over her ineffectual protests, and after a few shouted instructions to his coachman and outriders, followed her. "Wait," Gwynneth yelped as he sank into the luxurious squabs beside her. "Surely there is some other way than this precipitous marriage."

The carriage lurched forward in obedience to the sharp crack of the coachman's whip. In the light of the carriage lamps she could see that Langley looked deeply pained by her resistance. "Are you so unsure of me, then?"

"Of your sudden decision to marry me, yes. I don't want to find out later that you regret it."

"It wasn't sudden, Gwynneth."

"How can you say so, Stuart. Not moments ago you were offering me carte blanche, assuring me you'd left the carriage door open so as to avoid having to marry me."

"You still don't understand, do you? The carriage door

was left open for your sake, too, so you would have a choice and know that I had chosen, not been trapped."

"I played my part too well, I see. I had made up my mind it would be marriage long before tonight." He reached into his coat pocket and drew out a thick, crinkly parchment parcel, which he placed in her hands.

"What . . . what is this?"

"Since you would have a hard time reading by the carriage lanterns, you will have to trust me in this. In your hands is a marriage settlement. I had it drawn up day before yesterday in Kendal. An ancient solicitor and his clerks sat up all night preparing it and copying it."

"But . . . but I don't want, don't need a marriage settlement."

"Yes, you do, and I need for you to have it. It is the only way I could spare my conscience for bringing you into a legal form of slavery. It gives you an adequate income quite independent of me and my foibles, and the right to share custody of our children, no matter how grievously we might quarrel."

"But surely . . ."

"No, do not deny me this. Don't you see, Gwynneth, this way I can be sure I'll never let my temper trap me into tyrannizing over you the way my father did over my mother."

"Oh, Stuart. I don't believe you would ever do such a thing. You have the devil's own temper, at times, it's true, but it seems to pass quickly." She paused, reluctantly remembering her reservations.

"However, this trick you played on me tonight—that was no momentary temper fit, but a long-calculated act of vengeance."

"Which I would have put aside several times, gladly, if only you had spoken the truth to me."

"I just don't see how, if you love me and really want to marry me, you could have tormented me so."

"Because you were tormenting me with your standoffish

behavior. I deeply regret it now that I understand fully your reasons, I assure you."

He chuckled. "Do you remember John Donne's poem 'The Bait?' "

"Yes, but what does that have to do with . . ."

"You, my precious 'bait,' had caught me. This foolish prank was just the last desperate twitch of the trout before you reeled him in. But now you have landed me, and . . ."

"No! I don't want to 'land' you. You make me sound like the Ridgeways with their tricks and schemes. I want to be loved as I love, with no reservations." Gwynneth stiffened and moved as far from him in the carriage as she could. "Take me back. Lady Ridgeway will shelter me, I am sure, or . . ."

He closed the distance between them immediately and stopped her words with a brief, hard kiss. "Ha! You've admitted you love me, and thus sealed your fate. I'll not risk losing you to Barlow. I mean to marry you before the next sunset."

Another kiss, gentler, more coaxing. "Come now, Gwynneth. You know you can't hold out against me—else what was all this frantic hiding and masquerading about?" He slid his warm hands up her arms caressingly.

He knew her secret. She had confessed, and now he knew that her whole being seemed to yearn for union with his. And as she had always feared, that knowledge was powerful in his competent hands. Helplessly she clung to him as he began to make love to her, his hands stroking as his lips sought, his tongue probed.

At last she managed to gasp out her one final reservation. "Are you entirely sure you won't be ashamed to be married to a bookseller?"

A possessive light leaped in his eyes. "Then you will marry me!"

"Oh, yes, please."

In the soft glow of the carriage lamps Gwynneth could

see the joy that suffused Lord Langley's features. He gave her a final light kiss, then settled himself deep in the comfortable cushions and tucked her against his side, his strong arm holding her gently but firmly. "The baron and the bookseller. I like that. Perhaps we can bring out a book of poetry together . . ."

Epilogue

"**H**ere they are!"

Gwynneth looked up to see her husband eagerly waving a sheaf of papers as he strode toward her through the rose garden of their London townhouse. She set her writing aside and rose awkwardly to meet him.

"The galleys, at last, for *The Baron and the Bookseller*. Wait until you see how well our poetry looks, side by side." Beaming, Langley held the sheets out to her.

Gwynneth took the papers from him slowly, reluctantly. "They finished the typesetting so quickly? Then the book will come out before the baby arrives."

Lord Langley looked closely at his wife. "You're not pleased."

Gwynneth forced a smile to her lips. "Of course I am. I know how much you want to show the world that females can have merit as poets, and I'm very flattered that you value my work so highly." She read the galleys as she walked down the sun-dappled, petal-strewn path.

Langley silently paced beside her for a few moments, watching her as she read, then caught her elbow. "Sit a moment, Gwynneth. It is time we had a serious talk."

The golden eyes were wary as they met his. "What about?" But she allowed him to return her to the bench.

"You don't really want me to publish this, do you?"

"I want you to be happy. . . ."

"I am happy, just having you for my wife. It makes me unhappy to see a shadow across your face like this."

Gwynneth carefully set the sheaf of papers beside her on the bench before turning to her husband. "I want to please you, but I have to confess that publishing this volume makes me very uncomfortable."

Langley jumped up and began pacing frenetically. "I am an insensitive clod. You dislike being reminded that you were once a bookseller, and here I go shouting the fact to the whole world. And all because I couldn't resist a bit of alliteration. I shall change the title."

"No, dearest, it's not that. I'm not quite the snob I once was. Almost a year of meeting your many friends, from all walks of life, has vastly expanded my view of society.

"But once this book is published, it can't help but be widely noticed, because of your fame. My anonymity will be a thing of the past. When I lose my privacy, I fear I shall lose my freedom to write without inhibition. Being recognized as a poetess won't be worth what I will lose. I don't want to become a literary lion, like you. Fame won't suit me."

"*Lioness*—and with those golden eyes, you are perfect for the part."

"I'll be stared at, talked about, treated like a freak by some. Others will be watching to see if I can continue to write good poetry. I can picture them lurking like vultures, ready to pounce on future failures. Others will say you wrote my poems, or helped me."

Langley's expression darkened forbiddingly. "They'd better not."

"They will, though. And what about those poems which are opposed to your own opinions? Aren't you afraid that you will be ridiculed for being unable to control your wife?"

"It will serve to underscore my belief that women should be respected as individuals, apart from their husbands."

"And I would always worry about offending someone whose vote you are wooing for some reform measure in parliament. No, I fear that writing will be almost impossible when this book comes out."

"But Gwynneth, you won't be able to quit writing. Indeed, weren't you doing so when I joined you just now?"

"Yes, I was. This poem has helped me clarify my thinking on this subject. You see, this one is . . . well, different. And because I was worrying about how it might affect the way people treat me, or how it might damage your political aspirations, I began to feel that I could never publish it. Don't you see, I won't feel free."

"There's that word again. *Free.* I knew someday you'd resent the loss of freedom that marriage involves, but I'd hoped it wouldn't come so soon. Not even a year has passed, and already you regret . . ." Pain filled the chocolate-brown eyes which couldn't quite meet hers.

"There's nothing about our marriage that I regret." Gwynneth put her hands on her rounded abdomen. "The best poem I ever wrote or ever hope to write is in composition right now."

Smiling, he returned to her side and placed his own hands over hers. "You can't take all the credit for this little love poem!"

"This collaboration I shall joyfully acknowledge." She lifted her face for his kiss.

He sat beside her on the garden bench, enjoying the companionable linkage of their hands. "Well, if the book is to be a source of discomfort for you, I shall put it away. Perhaps someday our children or grandchildren will publish it. But your work deserves to be read and appreciated. I can't bear to think of your ceasing to write, or failing to publish."

"Nor *shall* I. Miss Suzanne Allen will continue to have a good deal to say to the world. Only Nicholas knows the truth, and he will keep our secret if you ask."

Gwynneth was rewarded by a look of joy on her husband's handsome face. "That's what you mean to do, then, continue writing under a pseudonym?"

"Yes, though if poems such as the one I was just working on are to be published, Miss Allen had best become a Mrs. Somebody, right away. Does this solution please you, Stuart?"

"There's almost nothing that you do that fails to please me." He bent his head to kiss her gently, tenderly. "Now let us have a look at Miss Allen's latest work. There is a dearth of good material for *The Legacy* this month."

She handed him the sheet and watched, a certain mischievousness in her golden-hazel eyes, as he read. When he had finished, the look he gave her was full of heat. "You are quite correct. Miss Allen must be given a husband, right away! And a fortunate man he will be, too."